Granny Samurai

Dear Reader,
In this book you will
find the true story of how
I met Granny Samurai, as
scribed by me and transgressed
to computer by Mr John Chambers
Esq. Enjoy!
Samuel Johnson

Granny Samurai,
the Monkey King and I

John Chambers

WALKER
BOOKS

First published 2013 by Walker Books Ltd
87 Vauxhall Walk, London SE11 5HJ

2 4 6 8 10 9 7 5 3

This book has been typeset in Brioso Pro

Printed and bound in Great Britain by Clays Ltd, St Ives plc

British Library Cataloguing in Publication Data:
a catalogue record for this book is available from the British Library

ISBN 978-1-4063-4096-9

www.walker.co.uk

For both my
excellent grandmothers

In the Beginning

Boris Hizzocks was a brute. He was big and hairy and smelled like a rhino who had just spent a hard day cleaning toilets. He was strong enough to crush apples in his hands. He could hang from a bar by his teeth.

Boris's mother Maddy was just as bad. When Boris was born, the doctor gave him a little slap. This doesn't hurt. It's to make the baby cry out.

Maddy said, "Punch him back, my lad."

And Boris did. That's how mean he was, even at that age.

In school he was bigger than all the
other kids. He stole their mobile phones
and laughed about it. He flicked spitballs at
their sweaters. He rubbed snot into their

hair. He never did
his homework,
and when the
teachers asked
about it, he
mumbled that the
dog had eaten it. (This was true by the way,
because he had fed it to him.)

All in all he was a terrifying personage
and most sane people kept well out of his way
if they could.

This is me. Sitting beside Boris at school.
I am sane, and I can tell you that it wasn't
the seat of my first choice. But I was new
to this school and the only empty place
was next to him. Big surprise.

My name is Samuel Johnson.
I am the scribe of this story.
The ancient Egyptians
had scribes who would
write letters and stories

for people in the marketplace. I am too young
to be an ancient Egyptian but I am still a
scribe. I am scribing this story for you. Later
I will tell you why. Although this story is not
actually about Boris, it commenced with him.
This is how.

On my first
day at the school
Boris boxed
my ears once.
He twisted my
arm twice and
gave me four dead legs. He practised
Chinese burning on my wrist, then pinched
his nose and blew snot all over my exercise
book. He had me in his fearsome
grip from first bell to last bell,
and because everyone else
was terrified of him too,
nobody said anything.

This is me.
Limping home.

ha ha

The following morning dawned bright and clear. Actually it was murky and foggy. The other sentence is from a book I'm reading.

I went downstairs and found a note from my Uncle Vesuvio. He'd had to go away in the middle of the night, he said, and I should get my own breakfast. There was a crisis in Azerbaijan but he would try to get home as quickly as possible. My uncle is a diplomat and often has to go away and be diplomatic somewhere. He is a "real gentleman". I put that in quotes ("") because that is what most people say about him. It is also what he is. But sometimes when you put something in quotes it means the exact opposite. For example, *Boris Hizzocks is a "real gentleman"* actually means that he is a complete thug and torturer.

That day Boris yanked my hair six times, poked my ear with a sharp pencil twice,  twisted my arm behind my back once and did milking the rat three times until finally the teacher noticed  and told him to pay attention.

"Yessir," he grumbled, still not letting go of my fingers.

"And you, new boy," said the teacher, "sit up straight and stop messing."

Messing! I hoped the teacher would get a new pair of glasses for Christmas.

This is me again. Limping home again.

I made my own tea. There was a postcard from my uncle to say that the crisis in Azerbaijan was coming to a head. In the meantime there was money in the freezer and lasagne in the sugar tin. He must have scribbled *that* postcard in a hurry. Later on I did the washing up. And what about *my* crisis? I thought whilst scraping bits off plates. What about that enormous savage beside me at school? I stared gloomily through my reflection into the dark back garden.

Outside, the old lady next door was chopping wood with her hand. I shook my head hard. All that frozen lasagne was going to my brain. She picked up her blocks and went inside. I switched off the light and went to bed.

The Next Day

The next day I was late for school. The
teacher made me stand in the corner, which
was fine by me as I was out of range of Boris.
I made up my mind to be late every single
day from then on. Then something small
and wet hit me in the back of the neck. Boris
was puffing chewed up bits of paper at me
through a biro. The bits were ripped
from one of *my* schoolbooks!
They lodged in my hair
like giant dandruffs
and I couldn't move

to get rid of them. The rest of the class sat in
uncomfortable silence. I was finding out what
they already knew: there was no escaping
his evil supremacy.

This is Boris,
chasing me home.
This is me, escaping. Luckily I am
fleet of foot, and being afraid
makes you go faster, too.

SMASH!

This is the sound that
Boris Hizzocks
makes when he
runs full-tilt into
a wooden gate
just opened by
the little old lady
next door.

"Whoops,"
she said, peering
up at him through
wrinkled raisin eyes.
"So sorry."
And closed
the gate again.

Before Boris
hit the ground I was
behind our hall door
and had triple-locked it.

From inside the house I peeped through the spyhole at Boris limping away. For such a little old lady she certainly knew how to open a gate pretty quickly. My uncle says that if someone does something nice for you, you should always thank them properly for it. So even though she did the nice thing by accident, I decided I would make a cake and take it over.

This is my favourite cake recipe:

4 eggs
150g castor sugar
150g white flour

Instructions
Beat the eggs and the sugar, and when
the mixture is foamy, fold in (which
means stir with a light hand) the sieved
flour. Eat it with a spoon.

The best thing about this recipe is that it is easy and you don't have to cook the cake. The mixture always tastes better than the cake anyway, and when I am an adult I believe I might open a shop only selling mixes.

Here's me, standing at my neighbour's door with a bowl of cake mix and a spoon.

I am keeping a sharp lookout for Boris Hizzocks and wishing she would hurry up and answer.

Then the door opened and for the first time in my life I was properly face to face with Granny Samurai.

The Faces of Granny Samurai: An Impression

Here is a drawing of how Granny Samurai appeared to me when I first saw her. Beside it is one of how she appears now. That's a funny thing I've noticed about people. They don't actually change, but somehow when you know someone well, they look different from when you first saw them. As you can see, she is small and her hair is tied up over her head in a bun. Her teeth are false and so is one of her legs.

Around her neck she wears a fur and in her hand she carries a walking stick that conceals a Black Centurion double-action repeater (of which there are only two in the world). In her handbag she has an ivory blowpipe that used to belong to Mahloomahwahoo, the fearsome pygmy king. She saved his life once and he gave it to her as a token of his gratitude. She has other weapons too, which I am not at liberty to reveal.

But like me back then, if you didn't already know this, you wouldn't learn it by looking at her.

"Yes?" she said, staring at me fiercely. "What you want?"

I held out the bowl and said, "Thank you very much for opening the gate at exactly the right moment." She looked at it suspiciously.

"What that?" she asked.

"That cake mix," I said. "I mean, *that's* cake mix. For you," I added.

She grunted something and coughed into her hand. Then she held out the biggest set of false teeth I had ever seen and said, "Take!" I took, and she grabbed the mix and gulped it down in less time than it took to write this sentence. (About four seconds.) Then she seized back her teeth and slammed the door.

"You're welcome," I said, and went home.

Saturday at Last

The next day I got up late because it was Saturday and there was no school. Saturday is the best day of the week because there is no school the next day either. Sunday is the second best. My big plan for the day was to read books and pretend I never had to go to school again for the rest of my life. The books at home were better than the books at school, in any case. I thought maybe I could pretend to be my uncle and write a note from his study to say that I was going to home educate me from now on. My uncle is a highly educated personage with top Internet access and an extensive encyclopedia collection. But how would I explain this to him later, when he got back from Azerbaijan?

I made a cup of tea and fried some sausages for breakfast. Like the Victorians, I am a great tea drinker. I read once that back then, tea was so expensive, they used the same leaves three times in a row, before passing them on to their poorer relatives. Victorians always had poorer relatives. I imagined passing on a wet tea bag to Boris Hizzocks, right in the face. It was a savoury moment until the picture came into my head of him passing it right back to me, with fuller force and enmity. I tried thinking about something else instead. Then the doorbell rang and interrupted my thoughts, which was fine by me.

I sneaked a look through the letter box just in case it was you-know-who, but it wasn't. I opened the door.

Outside, a tall adult in a yellow coat and a large Stetson hat stared right at me. He was wearing dark glasses.

"My uncle's not in," I said. The adult scratched his ear.

"What about your granny?" he whispered. He had a voice like matches being struck.

"I don't have a granny," I said.

"Everybody has a granny," he replied, and waited. Well, he had me there.

"I used to have a granny," I amended, "actually I used to have *two* grannies, but I don't have them any more. They were very ancient," I added, by way of polite explanation. He leant in closer.

"Tell your granny," he whispered, "that the Monkey King wants to negotiate." Then he turned and limped away.

The Monkey King! For a moment
I wondered if he was referring to Boris
Hizzocks. He was hairy enough to deserve
the title. Then I wondered if it was something
to do with Azerbaijan, except that was to do
with my uncle and not my granny, even if I
had had one. Finally I gave up wondering and
returned to my book. This new town seemed
to be full of weirdos, and when my uncle
returned, I decided, I would start a home
advertising campaign to go somewhere else
ASAP. ASAP is an abomination and means
AS SOON AS POSSIBLE. If there were more
abominations, books would be a lot shorter
and scribing wouldn't take up
so much time.

The doorbell
rang again.
This time
I opened it
without looking.

Big mistake. Boris Hizzocks was hulking outside.

"Hey midget," he sneered, "want to come and play?" And he snickered at me. I knew what he meant. I'd seen a documentary once where a giant gorilla played with a bug he was going to eat.

"No thanks," I said and shut the door. But Boris had jammed his foot in it.

"I know where you live," he grinned. Well that was pretty obvious. I put my shoulder to the door to push it closed but Boris just laughed. Then suddenly the laugh turned hollow and he jumped backwards. Something from behind me had just jabbed him hard in the toe.

OWA!

JAB!

"So sorry and goodbye," said a voice I'd heard before. Then the little old lady from next door reached around me and shut the door firmly in Boris's aghast mug. I turned to look at her.

"How did you get in here?" I asked, in amazement.

"You left the door open," she replied, in normal language. Then she headed for the kitchen. "My name is Granny Samurai," she said. "But you can call me Granny. I only drink cold instant coffee. If you don't have any, you'll have to get some in."

I followed her in a meek fashion.

A Secret Book

THE LOST SECRET ART OF KENJO by Granny Samurai explains quite clearly how to move secretly and swiftly through a door in the process of being closed – *without being seen!* To do this, you have to have accomplished

five things: **1.** Walking barefoot over a long sheet of rice paper, without leaving a mark, after your feet have been dipped in treacle. **2.** Catching a fly in mid-air, with chopsticks, by its back left foot. **3.** Shooting

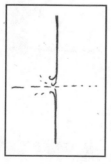

an arrow through a single hair in a dark room with your eyes closed. **4.** Writing your name with a sharp pencil, in one stroke, on a single grain of rice.

The fifth thing has been lost, hence the title of the book. Though when I asked Granny Samurai how it could be lost if she knew all about the lost art to begin with, she just grinned, which made me stop asking questions. Being grinned at by Granny Samurai is quite alarming. Her teeth are as big and yellow as old piano keys.

But this all came later. Right now I sat in the kitchen while she drank cold instant coffee and looked at me.

"Why do you drink cold instant coffee?" I asked.

"Because I don't have time for frills at my age," she answered, taking a big slurp. "Plus I'm a caffeine fiend."

"How old are you?" I asked curiously, but she just grinned and belched. Whatever else about her, her manners were appalling.

"Who hairy friend?" she asked suddenly.

I said that Boris was my sworn enemy but that he was uber-strong and I just tried to keep out of his way mostly.

"Bit hard to do that when he knows where you live," she suggested. Like I didn't know! "And your pal with the hat?" she asked. "What he want?"

"He isn't my pal either," I said. "He is a weirdo."

Granny nodded and took another slurp of coffee. "Weirdos won't water waiting wallabies," she muttered, and added, "that's an anagram." She sucked the coffee around her teeth for a bit. No wonder they were so yellow. Then she asked casually, "Did he say anything, the weirdo with the hat?"

I answered precisely, "He said, tell your granny the Monkey King wants to negotiate." As a scribe I have a very good memory for things people say.

"Does he now?" said Granny Samurai, and looked interested.

"Does who what?" I asked, but she ignored the question. Then without saying goodbye she finished her coffee and went home.

An Unpleasant Confrontation

On Sunday morning I woke up feeling queasy. It was because I knew I would have to face Boris again on Monday. The smelly orc wasn't just ruining my week, he was wrecking my weekend, too. There was no post from my uncle, either, to tell me about his massive crisis on the other side of the globe. I wondered whether he would be home before I ran out of frozen lasagne.

A knock on the kitchen window rattled my nerves and I instinctively crouched down. I am not a chicken, but so many odd things had been happening lately that I was completely on edge.

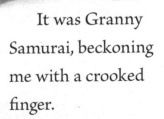

It was Granny Samurai, beckoning me with a crooked finger.

I opened the window and
she said, "I have decided you
need my help." Then
she pointed. Like
a giant ugly troll,
Boris Hizzocks
was perched on the
wall at the end of my
back garden.

He picked his nose when he saw me
seeing him and held up an oozy piece of snot.
"That's you," he bellowed, and ate it. "Yum

yum." My newly
adopted granny
shook her head.

"Genuine
suburban savage,"
she said. "*Typus
ultra dangerous.*"

Well, *that* I knew! My instincts screamed
at me to shut the window immediately. In
perilous situations, my uncle says, always

listen to your instincts. I went to do just that
but Granny Samurai blocked the window
with a special Kenjo block.

"The best thing to do is face him," she said.
I gulped, but it was a bit embarrassing to back
down from marching into the jaws of doom
with a little old lady watching.

"OK," I said in a weakened voice. "I will."

"Not you," she said, frowning. "You
haven't had the training. I'll take care of the
smelly intruder."

And she did.

I won't go into details.
Suffice it to say that the
noise Boris made as he
ran howling down the
street was the most
satisfying I had heard in
a long, long time.

The rest of Sunday passed the way a normal Sunday should: quiet, and even a little bit boring. I cleaned the kitchen and made an instant coffee cake mix and it was a big success. The recipe is the same as the other except you add a cup of strong instant coffee.

That night I slept soundly and had pleasant dreams. In one of them my uncle stood in the middle of a huge plain in Inner Azerbaijan. On either horizon armies were massing and shouting at each other. When he raised his hands they were quiet. "All together now," he said, and they did the chicken dance.

When I grow up I am not going to be a diplomat.

A Most Incredible Act
of Educational Injustice

On Monday Boris didn't come to school. There was a yawning vacancy beside me, which was very nice to look at. I hoped he had gone away to recuperate for aeons in Outer Bavaria or somewhere. Then the headmaster's voice came over the loudspeaker and

shattered my hopes.

"Samuel Johnson," he said. "My office. Now!" He's another one who rarely speaks in complete sentences. But his false teeth are better than Granny Samurai's.

That's me in the office. That's Boris's mother Maddy beside me. That's Boris beside her. The headmaster is opposite and you are about to witness the Most Incredible

Act of Injustice in the History of Education.

"This child," said the headmaster in thin tones. "Claims. You roughed him. Up."

"And down!" screamed Maddy Hizzocks, in a voice like chalk going through a cheese grater. "My Boris. My lamb. My ickle mickle Boris baby. My lad." And Boris smirked at me.

I knew exactly what had happened. He hadn't wanted to admit that an ancient granny had scared him half to death but he had been too stupid to stay scared. So when he'd got home, with nettles down his pants and a bloody nose, he had made up a story for his mother, who was now out for revenge.

"He pulled my Boris off a wall,"

screamed Maddy, even louder than before. "And bashed him up. Then stung him with nettles and ran away."

The headmaster glared at me. He was another one who needed glasses, because anyone who looked at us could see that the only part of that sentence that could be true was the running away part. In fact what had happened was that Granny Samurai had twisted Boris off the wall with a Niksu foothold, bounced him off the ground with a Shinsha shout and helped him back over the

wall (and into the nettles
on the other side) with
a Miso throw. Then
she had punched
a hole in the
bricks and
told him she
would pull
his leg back
through and
bite it off if he didn't get up and start
running right now. She had bared her teeth
when she said this and he had been halfway
down the lane before the sentence was over.
Granny one,
Boris nil.

So how
come I was the
one in trouble
now?

I tuned back in to the headmaster's annoying voice. "I have. No. Choice," he was saying. "But to. Suspend. The guilty. Party."

Good, I thought. The fact was, I had lots of other things to do besides being tortured to death at school by a hairy baboon – like reading, for example, or cooking. Maddy Hizzocks glared at me.

"Look at him," she said. "He's smirking. The least you could do is expel the brute."

I desmirked quickly and was doing my best to look dejected when the headmaster added, "This is a bad. Start. To your. School career. New boy Jenson. I will speak. To. Your. Uncle. About you. Dismissed!"

"Johnson, not Jenson," I wanted to say, but didn't. And Boris smirked, as now I really did look dejected.

*　*　*

That night I thawed out some more frozen lasagne. There were four left now and they weren't getting any more delicious. I hoped my uncle would be home before I had to start eating roots from the garden or something. Then I thought of what the headmaster would say to him when he got there and I wished he would stay away a bit longer. It wasn't that I didn't trust my uncle or anything, but grown-ups have a way of talking to each other sometimes where they leave out everything that is really important. PING!

The microwave pinged to tell me my lasagne was ready. I took it out and thought

I'd watch some TV while I ate. There was an old horror film playing on Channel One and I watched it for a while. A man was being chased by a creature that looked like it was made of microwaved lasagne. Bits fell from its face while it ran. Normally this would bother me a lot but now I just gave a hollow laugh. I knew what true horror was, and its name was Boris Hizzocks. I switched off the TV and went to bed early.

In the middle of the night I dreamt that a little noise woke me. It was a soft THUNK! from somewhere in the house, like a cat landing on a carpet. In my dreams a hairy face with red  cunning eyes stared through the window at me while I slept. It scratched at the glass like Hansel and Gretel but couldn't get in.

Then the phone rang and it vanished. I woke up.

It wasn't the phone. It was my alarm clock. I groaned, fearful of the frightful day ahead of me at school, then suddenly remembered that I didn't have to go after all. In fact I wasn't *allowed* to go. I jumped out of bed and the phone rang.

"Good morning. Junson," said the headmaster. "Could I. Speak to your. Uncle. Please."

I blanched and was hastily trying to think of what to say when a hand grabbed the phone from my fist, nearly giving me a heart attack in the process.

"Who this?" said Granny Samurai loudly, clacking her teeth into the receiver. "WHO?" she bellowed again as the headmaster shouted his name down the phone at her. "NEVER HEARD OF HIM AND NOT INTERESTED!" Then she hung up and waited.

"How did you get in?" I asked.

"Through cat flap," she answered.

I frowned. We didn't have a cat flap.

The headmaster called back.

Chapter nine of THE LOST SECRET ART OF KENJO by Granny Samurai is called "Flop Flop Fish in Frying Pan". The subtitle is Five Delicate Techniques for Exhausting Your Opponent.

Delicate is subjective, as you will see.

This is how the conversation went:

Phone: *RING RING.*

GS: HELLO, PLEASE.

HM: IS THIS. THE JOHNSON. HOUSE. HOLD?

GS: HOLD WHAT, PLEASE?

HM: DON'T HOLD, I...

GS: OK, BOSS.

She hangs up.

Phone: *RING RING RING RING.*

GS: WHO THERE?

HM: PLEASE DON'T HANG UP. I'M.

LOOKING TO. SPEAK WITH. VESUVIO
JOHNSON. PLEASE.
GS: WHO YOU?
HM: THIS IS THE HEADMASTER OF ST
ELMO'S SCHOOL FOR BOYS.

As you can see, the pauses between his words
were getting a lot shorter. Plus he was shouting
so loudly I bet the whole school heard him.

GS: ELMO NOT HERE.
HM: I'M ELMO ... I MEAN, *I'M* ELMO'S
HEADMASTER. I MEAN...
GS: MAKE UP MIND.
CALL BACK!

She hangs up again. I didn't
suppress a grin. If the head
had had any hair, he'd
have been tearing it
out by now.

Phone: *RING RING RING RING RING RING.*

GS: HELLO, YES?

HM: CANYOUASKVESUVIOJOHNSON
TOPLEASECALLSAMUELSSCHOOL
THANKYOU.

This is called "getting a word in edgeways".
In fact it is an entire sentence disguised as
a word. But if you are dealing with Granny
Samurai in exhausting-your-opponent mode,
you have to act fast. And I can tell you, it was
a nervous moment when he said it, too. But
Granny Samurai was ready.

GS: Why?

HM: *[Preliminary confused silence.]* Er ...
because Samuel is suspended. For ... er ...
bullying.

GS: Who say that?

HM: Other boy say it. I mean, *the* other boy
says it. Is this Samuel's uncle?

GS: This Granny. Who you?

HM: Headma— *The* headmaster.

GS: Uncle back weekend. Call then.

And she hung up.

We waited for the phone to ring again but it didn't. The minutes passed and I had a pleasant mental picture of the headmaster sitting in his armchair dabbing his bald head with a hanky. The last thing he wanted to do was call back and have another round.

"How do you know my uncle will be back at the weekend?" I asked suddenly.

"Postcard say so," Granny Samurai replied, pointing. I looked behind me down the hall. A postcard and some bills were being poked into the letter box as we spoke.

"It's rude to read other people's postcards," I said firmly.

"But it's interesting." She grinned. "Now follow me." I followed.

55

We went into the
back garden. No
Boris Hizzocks
this time.
"Look," she said.
I looked.

Over my head
a large twigsome
branch stretched out
from the walnut tree,
almost to my bedroom.
That must have been
what was scratching
my window the
night before.

"Not there," said Granny Samurai impatiently. "*There*." And pointed my head towards the ground. In the muddy grass at the tree roots I percepted tiny pointy handprints, as if a small creepy child had been walking around on its hands. The muddy prints continued up the trunk.

"The ... monkey thing!" I gasped, remembering suddenly what the weirdo had said. Then it *hadn't* been a dream, it had been here last night!

"Hee hee hee," wheezed Granny Samurai, with a noise like a boiling kettle only more alarming. "*King*, not *thing*. Hee hee hee." Then she turned serious. "Those not Monkey King prints," she said. "Those primals'."

"Primates," I corrected her, using a superior precision word for monkey.

"Primals," she retorted. "Monkey King servants called primals. But what primals want here?"

"Perhaps they were after the walnuts?" I said hopefully.

"Hee hee hee," snorted Granny again, and clapped me on the shoulder. She was still laughing as she vaulted back over the wall into her own garden.

I put some ice on my shoulder and spent the rest of the day reading my uncle's encyclopaediae. At least they told you things that made some kind of sense. That was Tuesday.

Wednesday

Wednesday started peacefully. I made a soothing hot chocolate and then I read the cartoons in the newspaper. My favourite cartoon is "Horrid + Ugg". It is excessively humorous and here is an example of it.

Next I did the crossword. I enjoy crosswords, though I am not as superior as my uncle at doing them. He is a crossword fanatic. There are two kinds of crossword clues. The first is easy like *male majesty (4)*, i.e. king. The second is hard, with hints of abstraction like *unlocking holy cage (6)*. You have to think around the corner. What unlocks something? A key, perhaps? Then you think holy, holy,

holy ... a shaman is holy. Or a monk? Then
you put it together and you get monk ... key.
A monkey! Which has six letters and could
be in a cage. King – monkey. I stared at the
crossword. Monkey King! With perplexed
brain (which means confused) I did the next
clue. *Average jouster (7)*. Average ... middling?
Who jousted? Knights of old! Knights ...
night; middling ... mid. Midnight! Monkey
King midnight. But midnight what?

A noise from the hall door made me jump.
It was the postman shoving letters through
the letter box. I went and looked. There
was another postcard from Uncle Vesuvio.
Whatever else about the Azerbaijanis, they
have a tip-top postal system. *Dear Samuel,*
wrote my uncle. *Will write more later. Your
uncle, Vesuvio.* Well
that was one of the
least inspired postcards
I'd ever read.

Then a loud voice from outside the door shouted, "KNOCK KNOCK."

"Who's there?" I asked automatically, when I'd recovered my composition.

"Santa Claus," snorted the voice with immense sarcasm. The way things were going lately I wouldn't have been surprised. I peeped through the peephole and Granny Samurai peeped right back at me. "Any more visits from you-know-who?" she whispered loudly.

"From Boris Hizzocks, you mean?" I whispered back.

"From other you-know-who?" she grunted.

"Ah," I said, "you mean the weirdo with the hat?"

"Mean hat, say hat," snapped Granny. "*Other* you-know-who!"

"The Monkey King?" I uttered. "Yes! Look here," and I opened the door to show her the crossword.

"No need," said a voice from behind me, and I turned around.

"How did you do that?" I asked in amazement.

"Easy peasy," she said, grabbing my paper. "Teach you later." She focused her gaze and read quickly. "*Monkey King, midnight. Summerhill Road 5.*
Hah!"

"Summerhill Road 5," I mused. Hmm. Interesting! Five letters. "Summer … summer, winter; hill … mountain… Wait," I stammered. "That's not a clue at all. That's my address." Granny pulled back her lips into a ferocious snarl and nodded grimly.

"Well done Sam," she said. "Brainpan cooking now. Cracked code like walnut. Monkey King coming 5 Summerhill Road at midnight."

"But," I asked, with growing unease in my innards, "why?"

Granny Samurai picked her ear and grinned. "Catch him, ask him," she replied. "Hello Monkey King. Why you attacking Samuel?"

"*Attacking me?*" I said, aghast (which means highly alarmed). "But why?"

"Interesting question number two." Granny grinned. "But don't worry. We have element of surprise plus major plan."

"Plan?" I uttered nervously. "What plan?"

Then she told me.

When I heard it, I am not ashamed to report that I turned excessively pale, then fainted. I am a scribe, you see, and not a warrior.

The Plan

HUNTING THE FEROCIOUS
TIGER by Ellington Smythe-
Worrington is the title of
the excessively thick book
that Granny Samurai was
fanning me with as I came out of my faint.
I read it later and can recommend it very
highly.

It is by the famous Ellington Smythe-
Worrington, who is no longer famous but
back in the mists of time was a well-known
Victorian big-game hunter. In his life
he shot and killed innumerable birds
and animals, and stuffed them for
his private collection. He was
nicknamed One-Shot Smythe
because he only ever needed
one shot to do the
dastardly deed.

His gun had a single chamber. But this was also his downfalling when the bullet he fired ricocheted off the horn of a large white rhino and hit a massive bull elephant in the behind while it was sharpening its tusks against an ancient baobab tree. By the time the bullet struck the elephant, most of the power had gone out of it and it only stung. But a good rule of thumb is not to sting bull elephants in the bottom and especially not while they are sharpening their tusks.

The elephant chased Ellington Smythe-Worrington for exactly six seconds before it caught him. Smythe-Worrington ducked behind a large tree to reload and the elephant went straight through it. When it had finished pounding him into the ground with the tree trunk, the elephant bashed the one-shot rifle to bits with a rock. Then it did a dance of jungle triumph on the hunter's remains while the bullets popped like firecrackers under its enormous feet. Then it did something even more unspeakable which I will not mention here in case a young person is reading, but think *manure*.

Over one hundred years later, the only surviving copy of this book was in the possession of Granny Samurai and being waved in my face. On the inside cover somebody had written, *To a great gal and granny, always yours, One-Shot.*

"Is that...?" I asked.

"Read," said Granny.

"But you can't be..." I said.

"READ," she barked, and shoved the book at my nose with a big thumb pressed down hard in the middle chapter. The nail was long and polished and crooked. I read.

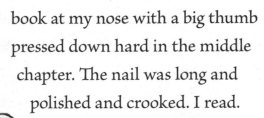

"To catch a tiger, stake out a goat. It should be a young goat, active and loud, with a good strong smell and a high

voice. Tie him firmly to a stake, then take your place in a nearby tree with a flask of good brandy and your weapon. Await the rustle of the bushes that precedes the arrival of the stripy horror. Should you plug him before he pounces, you may present the goat to the local tribesmen to roast in your honour. Should the tiger arrive at the goat before your bullet arrives in the tiger, a stew is recommended instead."

BONK!
BONK!

"Understand?" said Granny.

"No," I said.

"To catch tiger," she said, "use goat." She tapped my head with a hard knuckle. "Hello brain, bonk bonk."

"You mean," I said slowly, "we will set a trap to catch the Monkey King at midnight, using a monkey – I mean a goat – as bait, and somebody is the goat."

"Light bulb on long last," said Granny Samurai and looked intently at me. With sudden awful clarity I glimpsed the depths of her cunning mind and gasped in inward horror. I am a scribe, I thought, and not a goat. But though my uncle had taught me prudence, he had not raised me to be fearful. "Valour is a worthy goal," he would say. "Be brave." Still, I had other worthy goals in life so I opened my mouth to refuse, when to my horror my uncle's teaching took over and the following sentence came out:

"OK, Granny Samurai," I said, "I volunteer to be the goat."

"Ha!" she shouted, and smote me on the head with HUNTING THE FEROCIOUS TIGER. "No worry goat. Monkey King take bait.

 Granny take Monkey King. Chop chop."

"Chop chop," I answered weakly.

"Not *you* chop chop, Monkey King chop chop," she said, and grinned loudly.

My Last Will and Testament

I hereby and herewith and heretohence prescribe all my earthly goods, including my books, my iPad and my fountain pen collection, to be left to my Uncle Vesuvio on his safe return from diplomacy. Please take any library books back to the library and pay all possible fines from the money in the old coffee tin on the shelf.

At my funeral I would like "Ode to a Young Soldier" by Percy Williams to be read out and the following songs to be sung:

1 ....
2 ....
3 ....

Samuel Johnson Esq.

I left blank spaces for the songs because I couldn't think of any to write just yet.

Granny Samurai said, *"Shanghai Lily good song for funeral."* I looked at her. "Or *Maguire's Pewter Mug,"* she added. "If you like Irish music. Deedle deedle deedle dee," she hummed, banging her wooden leg on the kitchen floor. "Irish music good kitchen music."

THUMP!
THUMP!
THUMP!

74

"It's rude to read other people's wills,"
I said, a trifle tartly.

"I'm too old to be polite," she said, "and
anyway, it's rude to think you are going to die
when I am looking after you."

Well that cheered me up a bit and I
thought maybe I should throw away my last
will and testament.

Then she said, "give *me* books not uncle.
Uncle no time to read. Too busy being
diplomatic wherever."

"No," I said shortly, and she shrugged.

"OK, whatever. Rest
now, stake out later."

"You're not actually
going to stake me out…"
I started to ask, but
she was already
snoring.

That cheered me down again, and I turned back to my will. I am a neat person and it is an unorderly thing to die in arrears, which I wanted to avoid – and dying too of course.

List of Songs to Be Played at My Funeral

I Get Knocked Down (But I Get Up Again)
I Bet You Look Good on the Dancefloor
Shanghai Lily

P.S. It is amazing how quickly time speeds up when you are worried about something.

The Rest of the Day ...

... ticked by with
terrible speed.
I selected a book
to read from my
uncle's study but
the main character
was too heroic for
reading comfort.
Plus it was hard to

read with Granny fidgeting beside me.

"Books boring snoring," she snorted,
and went next door to watch television.

That was fine by me. I sat in my uncle's
study and exercised calm. My uncle's study
is my favourite room in the house. It is full
of books and mementoes of his career thus
far. He is a souvenir fiend. On the next page
is what his wall of ultimate mementoes looks
like. I can easily spend hours looking at it.
This is what I did now.

After that I went
downstairs to the kitchen.
The kitchen is my second
favourite room in the house,
although the frozen lasagne was
putting me off it temporarily. At
some point late in the evening I fell
asleep at the table and dozed. In my
doze I dreamt that I was plunging
towards a jungle from a great height.
The air was full of drumming and
monkey howlings. Beneath me, a
pit of spikes yawned in gruesome
greeting. Just before I struck, I woke.
Granny Samurai was jabbing me
with hard fingers.

"Wake up goat,"
she grunted.
"It's stake-
out time."

JAB!

MORE
HOT
CHOC

The Stake-Out

Here's me in the front
garden. The night is dark
and quiet. The streetlights
are on and there is a
full moon in the sky.
I am hanging out in
the garden being bait.
Thankfully I am not
actually staked-out per
se and have free range
of movement up to
the front gate and
wall. I feel like
something in
the zoo.

I prowl with extreme nervosity, thinking that somewhere out there the Monkey King is watching and somewhere behind me Granny Samurai is guarding. At least, she says she is. She is concealed in the bushes and as hard as I look, I can't see her at all.

Chapter nineteen of THE LOST SECRET ART OF KENJO explains how this is possible. *Empty mind,* writes Granny, *and form will be empty too.*

When I said I didn't understand, she said, "Stop moving = vanish. Busy busy, always being seen."

This wasn't too clear to me either and I pressed her further.

"Look," she said impatiently, "the human eye is trained by evolutionary precision to see movement. This comes from when we were hunters and had to see edible things running away from us. Gatherers on the other hand just walk about gawping for stuff on the ground. If you don't want anybody to see you, the first thing you do is stop moving. And that includes blinking. Capiche?" I capiched.

Now she was being still and invisible somewhere while I was prowling and unpleasantly visible. A sudden movement caught my eye and I turned to gaze. Beyond the gate, at the far end of the street, a tall figure with dark glasses and a Stetson leant out from behind a chestnut tree and peered right at me.

I pretended I was admiring the moon. Then Stetson took a step forward and I stopped pretending. I stared instead. Now he was shuffling towards me quickly with shakes and jerks, like someone dancing and hiccuping at the same time. His gaze mesmerized me to the spot and sapped my will to move.

Brace Brace

A rough voice hissed from the bushes behind me,

"Clear brain goat. Brace brace."

I brace braced and glanced behind for Granny. All I saw was a massive nothing. With both ears I listened to the soft slithery shuffle of Stetson getting closer. My heart went *patapatapatapata*.

Then the gate squeaked and Stetson loomed over me. One foot caught in the other as I tried to get away. I fell to the ground. Stetson twitched into the garden and reached jerkily towards my throat. His dark glasses were like pools of ink on a slice of white bread. I opened my mouth to scream but nothing came out.

Then I saw her.

Perched like an owl in the ivy on the front
of the house, Granny Samurai was poised
to pounce. One hand was drawn back as if
firing a bow and the other hand was fixed like
an eagle's claw. Her wooden leg was aimed
straight at Stetson and her mouth was wide
open. I suddenly saw that she had two sets
of teeth in her mouth, like certain sharks.

Were both false? I thought. Or only one?
Then Stetson clapped his hands to his ears
and doubled up in pain. I didn't know it then
but Granny Samurai was giving him the full
Silent Shriek of Animalistic Annihilation.
His glasses fell off and I gave a not-so-silent
scream of animalistic annihilation myself.
Behind the glasses were holes and I could
see the indigo night sky right through them.
Something large
flitted
across
the moon.
Stetson
turned and
stumbled
towards the
gate. There is
no explanation
for what happened
next.

What Happened Next

I jumped to my feet and rugby-tackled Stetson around the waist. *Be brave*, rang my uncle's voice in my brain. Stetson's coat collapsed like water into my arms. A crowd of monkeys poured out and ran screaming away in all directions. So that's why he walked in such a jerky way, I thought. There was no *he*, just a suit of clothes stuffed with simians. Some king! Then one of the simians kicked my nose hard as he wriggled out from under me. I lay stunned on the path as a fog of pain settled over my brainpan. *Ouch,* I thought, and struggled to my feet. A distant laugh sounded, not hee hee, but something eerily else. Monkey King one, Samuel Johnson nil.

And where was my so-called guardian when I needed her? I slammed the front door behind me. That was Wednesday.

Thursday Morning, Bright and Early

Dawn washed the kitchen in a pale light. This popped into my head when I sat down to my scribing on Thursday morning. I hoped the kick in the nose had not affected my style, as the sentence was excessively poetic and I am more factual in nature. Therefore I just made a list of what happened next.

1. Granny Samurai came round and laughed at my sore nose. "Hee hee hee," she laughed. "Nose red. Look funny." I replied stiffly that if somebody had kicked her on the nose, she wouldn't be laughing either. "Neither would he," she retorted. "Hee hee hee." She gave a laugh like a baboon on helium.

2. She made herself a large mug of cold instant coffee and drank it while I sulked. "You were brave to tackle the hat," she offered, but I was unbending.

3. She yawned and swished the coffee between her gums.

The silence thickened around us.

"Well, where *were* you?" I exploded. "What happened to 'Monkey King chop chop, Samuel no chop'?" I stopped shouting. It hurt my nose too much.

Granny Samurai shrugged largely. "Monkey King stay back," she said. "Watch what happen primals."

I thought of the large dark shape flitting across the moon and the eerie laugh, and even though it wasn't cold I goosebumped slightly. The hat hadn't been the Monkey King after all.

Granny Samurai drained her mug and belched. "No matter. If all battles won always, no need for war. Meet fourteen hundred hours (which means two o'clock) in front of zoo." She grinned and held up something green. "Found zoo ticket in captured coat,"

92

she said. "Big fat clue.
Good job Samson."

I felt a tickle of pride but suppressed it. "*Samuel*," I said grumpily. "And what if the headmaster sees me?"

"Who cares?" said Granny Samurai. "Suspend from school, not zoo!" Then she left.

4. The post came while I was tidying up. There was a postcard from my uncle. He wrote, *Dear Samuel, situation much improved here. Maybe I can make it home before the weekend after all. Uncle Vesuvio.*

Well that would be nice.

5. The doorbell rang.

6. I nearly made the mistake of answering it. This is what I saw when  I looked through the peephole. Like most peepholes there is a lens in it that makes people look funny when you see them through it.

This is what Boris Hizzocks looks like through the peephole.

This is what Boris Hizzocks looks like with normal eyesight.

As you can see, he is in fact better-looking through the peephole.

He rang
the doorbell
again, then
bent down
and shouted
through the
letter box.

"Hey worm, I brought you your school lunch," he lied, then snickered. "Now open up!"

Open up? I thought, marvelling at his invincible stupidity. I would rather open up to a grizzly. I commenced backing silently down the hall. THUMP THUMP THUMP! Boris commenced thumping on the door. BOOM BOOM BOOM! went his fist, and the door shook horribly.

"Your granny left," he shouted. "I saw her getting on the bus to town. *Bok bok bok!*" he screamed. "Little chicken needs his granny to protect him. *Bok bok bok.*"

It took me a moment to realize that *bok bok bok* was meant to sound like a chicken and was an insult aimed at me. Other kids, I thought, played football at lunchtime, or swapped computer games. So why was I this ogre's lunchtime entertainment?

The letter box creaked again, and I could practically see his lips protruding through it. "Hey worm," he warbled, and his stinky breath filled the hallway. "I'll be waiting for you. Hur hur hur." Then a hairy ear pressed up against the slot and listened hard for an answer.

I desisted a reply and tiptoed away with

immense decisive silence. In ye olden days I would have gone upstairs and emptied the deep fat fryer on my enemy's head. But that wasn't allowed any more.

Nowadays I was constrained by civilization. "Civilization," says my Uncle Vesuvio, "is constraint." Also, I had an appointment.

Thus I slipped intelligently through the back door, over the back wall and out through the back lane. Two streets later I located a taxi with its light on. Like Caesar I hailed it and jumped in. It cost six pounds  fifty not to have to wait at the bus stop in full view of the aforementioned barbarian of the century, and was worth every penny. Constraint is good but retreat, when constraint is not an option, is very excellent.

The Zoo

This is the taxi pulling up in front of the zoo. You can study the picture as hard as you like and you will not see Granny Samurai because she is blending in and does not want to be seen.

That's
me getting
out of the taxi.
There is a single
pigeon watching me
balefully from the top of the
main entrance. The gate is chained
and padlocked. According to the sign, the
zoo is closed on Thursdays. The plaza outside
is completely deserted. In the corner near
the fountain a mini whirlwind twirls some
rubbish in the air. There is always
rubbish left
behind when
the visitors
are gone.

ZOO
OPEN 10 AM - 6 PM
EXCEPT THURSDAYS
SO HARD CHEESE TO YOU
Signed Management

This is Granny Samurai, appearing beside me.

I jumped with startitude and opened my mouth to ask her whence she came, but she shushed me. Then I started to tell her about Boris's visit but she shushed me again. Finally, I pointed out that the zoo was closed on Thursdays and she turned around and pinched my ear hard. Suddenly my lips went numb and I found I couldn't talk any more. She pinched my ear again and my lips came back. It felt like after the dentist when the feeling comes back slowly from the injection.

"Chit chat later," she snapped, and pointed her hand at the heavy padlock on the main gate. She scrunched her face in concentration and I was reminded of  how a baby looks when it is exsqueeging a poo into its nappy. Then the padlock fell open and so did my now non-numb mouth.

"How did you…?" I asked, but she had already pushed open the gate and walked inside.

"Hurry up," she said, and to emphasize the hurrying, she grabbed my jacket and hauled me along after her.

A Word About Zoos

I like zoos. Some people say that they are cruel to animals and maybe that is true for some species, like leopards or cheetahs,

which can run at sixty kilometres per hour
and are the fastest animals in the world on
legs and consequently need a lot of space (for
braking and such). But other animals, like
marmites, which live in burrows and never go
out because they are too nervous, on account
of which their cages always seem empty
when you visit, do well *in* zoos. However
they are not good *for* zoos because they seem
boring compared to leopards and cheetahs
and people don't go to see them as much.
This is because modern man is "hooked on
excitement" due to watching too much TV.
That's what my Uncle Vesuvio says, anyway.
TV today is full of action shots and close-ups
that make you feel like you are right beside
the lion mauling the zebra, for example.
In reality these are filmed from
about two miles away with a
lens as big as a dustbin and
the lion doesn't

even know it is being watched. (Which is just as well for the filmer, probably.) But when people who are "hooked on excitement" go to zoos, they are disappointed to see a dusty old lion in a cage doing nothing at all. Until they look closely and see how big it really is and how long its incisives are and how neatly their heads might fit into its mouth and then it all gets quite exciting again.

Once I saw a lion in a zoo roar so loudly that several people's hats fell off and one unpleasant family who had been throwing peanuts at it (in spite of a sign with instructions not to) nearly had a joint heart attack and I thought it served them right. It is bad to feed animals in the zoo and they had been warned also.

"Serve peanut brains right," muttered
Granny Samurai and I shot her a look.
Had she just spoken into my thoughts or had
I imagined it? "Imagined it," she grunted.
"Now focus. What you notice?"

I looked around. A sign said we were
heading towards the monkey house, and
another pigeon perched on the sign
stared at us balefully. Or was it
the same one from the gate?

MONKEY
HOUSE

SNAKES

Sniff
Sniff

"Same bird yes," breathed Granny, and aimed her own gimlet beadies at it. It jerked its head and stayed supremely silent. I couldn't blame it. I would have stayed supremely silent if she'd aimed her gaze at me. Then I realized what I should have noticed. *Everything* was supremely silent. We were standing in the middle of the zoo but there was no noise whatsoever. No yapping. No yowling. No yonking. (Tapirs yonk.) No anything.

"Animals watching," said Granny Samurai quietly before I could enquire. "Watching watching waiting."

"Watching what?" I whispered, guessing the answer even as she spoke it.

"Us," she said, and swung her head from side to side like a snake deciding where to strike. And all around, from every bush, cave, rock and hole, a thousand eyes of different shapes, sizes, ages and colours all bent in our direction. A deep-freeze shiver shuddered up and down my spine.

We walked on towards the monkey house.

"But why?" I whispered with extreme quietness, unnerved to be gazed at so powerfully.

"Because of what is going to happen," muttered Granny Samurai.

"And what is going to happen?" I continued with fearful rectitude, not wanting to know but needing to find out anyway.

"Something exciting," said Granny, and clacked her teeth together three times.

"Is that good or bad?" I asked next.

"We'll know when it's over," she replied.

Welcome to the Monkey House

The front part of the enormous monkey cage was empty. An old dead tree with a lone tyre hanging from it for the monkeys to play with was bolted in its centre. At the back was a small door that lead to the inside part.

"Keep watch," grunted Granny, and as I looked around to watch, I heard a sharp PENG! from the cage. I looked back and there was a bar missing. "Squeeze in quick," she said, and helped me vigorously, then followed. She put the bar back in place and marked it with a piece of thread pulled from her coat. "Escape route number two," she said, and winked.

"Where's escape route number one?" I asked. In answer she pointed to the small door

at the back. Beyond it, the inside part of the monkeys' cage was littered with pieces of fruit and monkey poo. It smelled like it looked. I said, "But even if we escape into there, we're still in a cage."

Granny Samurai said, "Inside, outside, no matter. Matter only what side."

"What side of what?" I asked.

"What side he's not on," she replied, and pointed behind me.

This is me looking.

This is what I saw...

The Monkey King Revealed

Adults are fond of saying that when you confront the thing you are most fearing, it is not actually as fearsome as you feared. I can reliably report that when it came to the Monkey King this was not the case. In fact, he was more fearsome than fear itself. In fact, I froze in the moment, and if a vampire had attacked me just then he would have cracked his teeth on my icicled blood. My toes clenched in my sneakers. My hairs went straight up in defiance of the immutable laws of gravity. My stomach sank like a lift.

The Monkey King stared right at us. And what a stare! His eyes were violet and shot with yellow streaks. His feet were hairy and size sixty. It looked like he had seven toes. His fingernails were red and sharp and curved like a Gurkha's knife. His hair, of which he had masses, was a horrible red. And lastly, he smelled like Boris Hizzocks after a

good rub-down with mouldy ancient cheese.
Around him, his smaller monkey servants,
the primals, preened and pointed. One waved
his foot and gibbered at my nose. I turned to
run, but Granny Samurai grabbed me.

"Hold the line," she
snapped. In fact, it was my hair
she was holding, and I fully
admit that had it not been for her
fearful grip I would already have
been through escape routes one
and two and still running.

Holding the Line

We held the line and the Monkey King
advanced. With one hand Granny Samurai
twisted me swiftly behind her back and
pinned me fast. With the other she made an
eagle claw and, crouching suddenly,
pointed it and her wooden leg
at our oncoming enemy.

Opening her mouth she unleashed upon him the full Silent Shriek of Animalistic Annihilation. Immediately all across the zoo a clamour of shrieking and hooting and yapping went up. Cages rattled and windows shuddered. In the distance I heard breaking glass, and one after another the lanterns on the paths outside exploded.

With a clanging noise, escape route number two toppled from the cage and clattered to the ground. I pressed my fingers to my ears and winced excessively. The Silent Shriek went on for longer than anyone human could possibly breathe. When she finally stopped, I almost felt sorry for her simian foe. I peered around her to percept his unconscious body.

The Monkey King was smiling.

If I'd thought that Granny Samurai had a scary smile, I learnt then what truly frightening meant. His teeth were solid gold and bigger than clothes pegs. I could see his purple gums. In a move so fast it blurred, he shaped one massive hand like a cobra, then folded one foot behind his head like a scorpion's pincer. Then he drew a vast breath and his hair stuck up in spikes behind him. I noticed something blue and yellow protruding from between his shoulder blades.

"Brace brace!" screamed Granny, and I braced, face pressed into the back of her coat. One second later the Monkey King enfolded us in a Non-Silent Howl of Ultimate Destruction.

With a sound like a firework exploding in a pig farm the world destructed around me. The bars of the cage blew apart like toothpicks. The bricks shattered as if hit by a hammer. Bits of fruit and monkey poo flew into the sky and the tyre dangling by its rope lashed about in a frenzy.

Granny Samurai shook a diamond-tipped claw from her sleeve and slashed it into the ground. "Hang on!" she shouted, which was the most unnecessary advice I had ever received. I hung on.

The Monkey King advanced. His Non-Silent Howl howled even louder. The noise of the animals in the zoo grew louder too.

Granny's claw squealed like a fork on a greasy plate and we started slipping backwards.

"Hold my umbrella!" she bellowed in my ear.

"What?" I bellowed back.

"Umbrella," she roared. "Hold umbrella and wait for order."

I took the umbrella and twisted the strap around my wrist. "What order?" I shouted, and Granny kicked the release button with her foot.

"Vamos!" she screamed, and I might have screamed as well. With a loud SNAP! the umbrella opened and the two of us were hurled up into the sky like a scrap of paper. The zoo and the Monkey King receded backwards away from us. Like the situation before, I would only know if this was good or bad depending on what happened next.

What Happened Next

This is me. I am clinging tightly to Granny Samurai, who is clinging tightly to the umbrella. (Good.) She is laughing. (Not so good.) We have just cleared the zoo wall and are as high as a five-storey house (Unclear.) The umbrella breaks. (Incredibly bad.)

This is us, falling through the air.

This is the tourist bus we land in.

Lidbury & Paynter

These are the tourists from Japan and Germany taking photos of the granny from the sky and her wobbly companion.

Using the remains of her umbrella as a hook, Granny swung herself and myself down from the bus and into a taxi.

"Five Summerhill Road snap snap," she said to the driver, who looked very much like the same one who took me to the zoo. We sped away quickly. It cost nine pounds twenty to get us home this time, even though we took the same route exactly, but I was too tired to say anything, or even care. And because I was too tired to care, I wasn't watching my back, either. These days, always a big mistake.

Big Mistake With Pleasant Outcome

The taxi pulled up at home. We got out. The seventeenth chapter of THE LOST SECRET ART OF KENJO says, *Never let your guard down.* That's all it says. It is excessively pithy.

As I was paying the taxi, and simultaneously letting my guard down, a great grubby golem jumped out of the hedge and attacked me.

"I told you I'd be waiting, worm," he roared, then screamed as Granny Samurai caught him with a pincered fist and swung him into the back of the taxi.

Without thinking, I reached in and gave

him the ear pinch she had worked on me.

"*Mmmm mmm mmm,*" went Boris, suddenly not able to talk.

"The city dump," I said to the taxi driver, "and quickly."

"*Mmmm mmm mmm,*" said Boris as the taxi sped away.

Granny Samurai clapped me on the shoulder and nearly broke it. "Megawocka!" she said. "That's Jabinesish for well done."

"Why can't you just say 'well done'?" I asked.

"Too easy," she replied. "And besides, you just learnt something new."

That was true, and as a scribe I have a professional interest in words, even from other languages.

The other nice thing about this chapter is that the big mistake was Boris's and not mine. Megawocka!

Thursday Evening

We went into the kitchen. "All best plans cooked up in kitchen," said Granny Samurai. "Stir stir, bring everything to boil quick quick."

As I found out later, she is a supreme planner but a rotten cook.

"Plus I'm starving," she said. She jerked open the freezer door and looked inside. "What that?" She hummed, and licked her false teeth loudly with a large red tongue.

"That's frozen lasagne," I said. "I can thaw one out for you if you like."

"I like it frozen," she said. "It's nice to suck and lasts longer."

Well she had a point there. For a moment I dwindled on the possibility of opening a shop selling frozen dinners on a stick. Right next to my non-cooking bakery. When I was older and had more money I would have to think about this some more. But now there were other matters to consider. The intrepinurial would have to wait.

"You bet," said a voice in my head.

I looked at Granny Samurai. She had bitten off a golf-ball-sized lump of frozen lasagne and was masticating it with her molars. Her dark eyes regarded me. Later on I knew this to be her thousand-yard stare,

but back then

I sometimes wondered if maybe she had fallen asleep. Except for the masticating, that is.

I then wondered what Uncle Vesuvio would do in my situation. Probably he would advise me to talk to the Monkey King to find out what he wanted. That would be the civilized thing to do. Granny Samurai snorted and a pea-sized piece of cheese flew out of her nose.

"Civilized!" She cackled.

I said suspiciously, "Can you *hear* what I am thinking?"

She gave me a big yellow grin, then took out her teeth and clacked them together in her hands. *Boo!* she ventriloquized in my head without making a sound. Then she stuffed her teeth back in and waved any

questions away. "Time to snooze," she said. "Ask questions later."

"*Snooze?*" I aghasted. "When the Monkey King knows exactly where we live?"

"Correction," she interjected. "Monkey King know where *you* live. But don't worry," she added. "Only visit nights. And Granny take first watch." She closed her eyes and commenced snoring.

Darkness Falls Across the Land

This is a line from an ancient song my Uncle Vesuvio used to hum when diplomacy was getting difficult. I thought of it now as I retreated to his study under the full-frontal assault of Granny Samurai's snoring.

It was true now
also. Outside the
window the garden
was growing
dark and dank.
I wondered how
Boris was getting
on at the rubbish dump.
With any luck he had been
recycled into something pleasant.
I thought about the Monkey King.
The shock of his reality was starting to
ebb and I wondered if I should phone the
police or something. *Hello, this is Samuel
Johnson and I want to report that I broke into
the zoo today, and the monkey cage, with an old
lady and nearly forfeited –
which means gave up
– my life to a giant
monkey with red hair
and golden teeth.*

Happily I escaped intact. Please investigate.

Or maybe not. I looked at the phone and thought again. Maybe I should *compose* my presentation first, *then* phone. "Diplomacy is the art of telling the truth carefully," says my Uncle Vesuvio, to which I add, "especially when you are dealing with so-called grown-ups." But my uncle was not exactly there to advise me; instead he was advising hostiles

in Azerbaijan. I looked at his latest postcard. *Situation much improved here. Maybe I can make it home before the weekend after all.* Well *my* situation wasn't exactly improving. I was starting to wonder if I would even survive until the weekend. I flipped over the postcard. "Juksli" was printed on it, and above that a picture of a happy nomad in traditional dress doing something nomadic with his yak. At least I thought it was a yak. But maybe it was the juksli. Or was the nomad called Juksli?

I laid the postcard down. Behind me on the study wall a clock mooed gently. The clock was shaped like a cow, with eyes that swivelled while it ticked. It had been a long day and my eyes were starting to swivel also. Outside, the dark trees vanished slowly against the dark sky. Downstairs, Granny Samurai snored like a bullfrog. I took up my pen and started thinking about composing. *Dear Police Commissioner,* I scribed, and hesitated. Hesitance in scribing is not my normal manner but it had been a long day. At some point the mists of snooze descended. I tried with feebleness to whisk them away but I suppose I must have slept.

Night Time: The Warrior's Dark Helper

This is the title of the fourth chapter of THE LOST SECRET ART OF KENJO as narrated by Granny Samurai.

The night is a gift, she writes, *to the tactical mind, because it strips your opponent of his*

advantages. If he has good eyes, now he is blind. If he is asleep, you can creep up and bash him on the conker. And if he is susceptible to night fears, you can play on them like a piano.

"What are night fears?" I asked later, whilst scribing it under her dictation.

el sueño
de la Granny
produce
monstruos

after Goya

"Fear of shadows, fear of what's under the bed, fear of bad dreams and fear of someone creeping up while you are sleeping and bashing you on the conker," she cackled.

"Do you ever have bad dreams?" I asked.

"Once," she said. "Long time back. But I entered my dream and tamed it."

"You mean you confronted the thing you were afraid of," I said, "and then you weren't afraid of it any more?" This was a bit like the philosophizing of my Uncle Vesuvio and I was surprised to hear it from Granny Samurai.

"I mean I confronted the thing I was afraid of and made it afraid of me," said Granny grimly, then grinned. "Much simpler that way."

I slept profoundly until morning. At some point the cat flap flapped and I awoke. I was lying in my bed. Outside the window pleasant melodies of birdsong sounded and I felt exclusively refreshed.

The horrors of the last few days, including Boris Hizzocks and the Monkey King, seemed like ancient memories to me. I put on my slippers to go downstairs.

"Samuel," said a familiar voice, and I turned around. "I told you I'd be back by the weekend," said my uncle, also wearing slippers, and standing in his study door. His slippers were dog-shaped, the same as mine, and he was very fond of them. I had saved up to present them to him two years ago when he crossed the threshold into old age by turning forty. He held out his arms and I took a step towards him.

"Wait," he said, stepping oddly backwards into the study and pointing at his wall of ultimate mementoes. "Do you think you can get that down for me?" "That" was a sort of ancient wicker tennis racquet, or maybe badminton, without strings, but cobwebbed.

I got it down and swished it, thinking how light it was and pondering why my uncle had simply called it "that". My uncle is a superior verbal precisionist and the "that" was very unlike him. My pondering expanded with his next sentence. "Now why don't we go outside and, er … play," he said.

"Play what?" I enquisited politely. My uncle is more a newspaper-over-coffee than playing-games-outside type of man.

"Oh … games," he said with airy imprecision. "Now come on. You go first."

He pointed towards the door but I was suddenly distracted by his slippers. The dogs' heads had expanded and sprouted long red teeth. A strong whew of rhino mixed with wet dog whiffed me on the nose. I stood at the study door and hesitated greatly. Sudden fear singed my innards.

Then a distant voice behind me shouted, "DUCK, STUPID, DUCK!" I wheeled and looked. At the other end of the landing, coat-tails flying in all directions, Granny Samurai erupted through the floor, her dark eyes flashing and her lips pulled back in a grimace of pure focus. In one hand she held her Black Centurion double-action repeater

with the barrel pointed right at me. The black
metal hole pinned my gaze and I stared with
red alert as it crackled into action. Green and
purple sparks flamed from its muzzle and
I ducked with immensity. I felt the bullets
whizzing past me, plucking at my
hair and clothes.

"Uncle!" I shouted with
automatism, but I knew it was
too late. I twisted round just
in time to see him crumple and
stumble. The bullets struck with
ferocity but exploded on contact into
puffs of sparkling dust. He seemed to
shrink and grow at the same time.

His eyes went orange and glarey.

His mouth split wide and hot and his teeth
turned golden. Something yellow and blue
glimmered between his shoulders. Behind
me Granny Samurai advanced, Black
Centurion blazing in her fist.

"WAKE UP GOAT!" she was shouting, but her voice was tinny like it was coming from the earphones of somebody sitting beside me. The bullets sizzled past. With sudden startling insight I remembered the cat flap flapping and realized that I was dreaming.

Wake up, Samuel, I thought, and concentrated hard. "WAKE UP, BRAIN!" I screamed. And I awoke.

It was morning.

I was standing in my uncle's study like a Grecian statue with one hand extended as if it had been holding on to something or other. A spear, or an offering to ye gods perhaps. In a chair by the window Granny Samurai was putting something in her bag and zipping it shut. On her lap was her Black Centurion double-action repeater. The chair beside the desk was lying on the floor and on the wall behind me the cow clock mooed nine times. From the front door downstairs came the sound of the newspaper being delivered.

"Nightwatch over," grunted Granny Samurai with satisfaction, folding her weapon and stowing it out of sight. "Goodbye night. Hello breakfast, coffee, day."

I can report with one hundred per cent accuracy that that was the worst night's sleep I had ever had.

A Note for the Observant Reader

Here is my uncle's study. There is his desk and the letter I was scribing to the Commissioner of Police. As you can see, I am leaving the study and not yet noticing the thing I should have noticed. If you compare this drawing to the one on page 78 you will perhaps notice it for yourself. If you do, then you are certainly more awake than I was at this time.

In my defence, maybe you have had
a better night's sleep.

Breakfast

*The newspaper that morning looked like a
tongue sticking through the hall door.* This is an
artistic way of writing and very atmospheric.
However, it is too flashy for me. But Granny
Samurai recommends it because it puts
more oompf in the text. If Boris Hizzocks'
tongue had been sticking through the letter
box I could have closed it with excruciation.
That would have put more oompf in the
text too. But it wasn't and I didn't. Instead
I pulled it out (the newspaper not the tongue)
and followed Granny into the kitchen. She
switched on the radio to KRW Mega Hit
Factory, *All the Greatest Hits of All Time,
Always!* I switched it to Radio 4 instead. I am
more a fan of factual programmes and not
music while I am in the kitchen.

"Boring snoring," grimaced Granny, stirring instant coffee powder into a mug of cold water. "Music much better."

"It's my radio," I said with rhetorical irritation. The bad dreams of the night before had made me edgy.

"Sport radio then," tried Granny. "KRW Your 24-Hour Sporting World, *All Others Are Losers!*"

"No," I said stiffly.

"Whatever," she retorted and rinsed her gums loudly with coffee.

"Must you slurp?" I said.

"I must," she answered, and stared at me through dark eyes. "Sammy cranky today," she cackled. Well so what?

I made myself a Vesuvious. A Vesuvious is orange juice with a red fizzy vitamin tablet added. It is named in honour of my uncle, who invented it. It is the second best cheerer-upper I know, after a soothing hot chocolate with cream. Then I thought I would make a hot chocolate also, as who knew what the fates had fated for me this morning. Well the fates did, I suppose, but knowing *them* it probably wasn't anything easeful.

Granny Samurai finished her coffee and put her mug down. "Sam stay home today," she said. "Relax. Hang. Duck down."

"Stay low, you mean?" I quizzed suspiciously. "Keep out of sight?"

141

"That too," agreed Granny and grinned. "Duck, stupid, duck," she quoth, then patted her handbag. "Must go now. Busy busy today. Big match starting. Uncle back later from Azerbaistan. Everything bonza!" She laughed and turned it into a sneeze.

"Azerbai*jan*," I corrected with suspicion. And what was she so cheerful about, anyway?

"Stan, Jan," grunted Granny, "whoever!" She stood up to go. "Friday Sports Round-Up on soon," she said. "Megawocka!"

"Wait," I said. "How do you know my uncle's back today?"

"Postcard say so?" She shrugged.

"It's rude..." I started uttering.

"Yeah yeah blah blah," she replied, and exited the back door. "Oh," she said, popping her head back in. "Stay home today means stay home today. OK? Spell on house, good for twenty-four-hour protection. After that, every Sam for himself!" She winked and withdrew.

"Smell?" I shouted, insulted. "This house does not smell! It is extensively clean and tidy."

"SPELL!" she roared from outside. "With P. To keep you-know-who away."

"And what if it doesn't keep you-know-who away?" I roared back.

"Then call me!" she shouted, getting fainter, and a scrap of folded paper flapped back through the closing door and landed on my palm. I opened it. In the middle was a telephone number scribed in tiny letters.

"I don't have a mobile," I called after her in exasperation.

"Stay home don't need one," came the reply. Then there was silence.

FLAP!
FLAP!
FLAP!

Silence

Silence is good when your brain is buzzing with information overload. It is useful for:

    A. shutting down your head hard drive

    B. composing your thoughts

    C. scribing them out

Scribing out thoughts as a list is a way of working out what you are thinking. It is a high class recommendation of my Uncle Vesuvio's.

Here is the list of the thoughts I scribed out:

1. "Duck, stupid, duck," quoth Granny Samurai, then laughed as she left to watch Friday Sports Round-Up. But how could she quote herself from my dream?

2. When I picked up the newspaper, a postcard fell out. *Dear S,* wrote my uncle. *C u sune. V.* "V"? That was more like a text than a postcard. And since when couldn't my uncle spell?

3. Most sinister of all, why had I awakened *standing* in the study door, one empty hand held out before me like Cicero the orator? Had I in fact been holding something in that hand, and if so, what? Or worse, had I become a sleepwalker, and if so, when? This particular thought greeted my bowels with an extremely queasy squeeze.

4. What about the "that"? Had I dreamed about the "that" as well?

I studied the list. Number four was the only question I could answer. Either I had taken down the "that", or I hadn't. I turned and plodded upstairs. The plodding because I wasn't sure if I really wanted to know the answer.

That!

The "that" was missing. Here is a drawing of where it is missing from. As you can see, the wallpaper underneath is darker, which means it must have been hanging there for a long, long time. Not any more!

I quailed as I realized that I hadn't really been sleeping. In fact the Monkey King had tried to seize control of my actions through my dream while Granny Samurai

battled him away. She could have pre-warned me about that, I thought. A dream is private and others have no right to break in and enter it. On my uncle's desk the letter to the Police Commissioner lay unfinished. I sat down quickly and picked up a pen. Once more my hand hesitated above the page. Here's why.

Dreamfighting: The Lost Secret

Chapter one of THE LOST SECRET ART OF KENJO by Granny Samurai is about dreamfighting. This is an ancient subversive technique which can only be used by the most highly initiated. "Initiated" is a precision superior word. It means those to whom something has been shown. What these things are is a secret; that they have been lost makes them even more secret. Granny

Samurai, however, has promised that she will speak of them later, and that I may then scribe some down. "When is later?" I asked then, as my curiosity had been tickled.

"Later," she replied, "is now plus time." This was an excessively pithy answer, and also very true. She still has to tell me!

Except I didn't write any of this because I didn't yet know about it. In fact I still don't one hundred per cent. Now I sat in the study and tried to explain to the Police Commissioner something that I didn't fully understand myself. I threw the pen down, suddenly very irritated with everything: with Granny, with Boris, with the school, with the frozen lasagne, even with Uncle Vesuvio. The last thing might have been a bit unfair.

The doorbell rang. I ignored it. The doorbell rang again, longer this time. And there was another noise too. I went and looked over the banisters and recoiled.

Down at the letterbox, what looked like a bunch of thick grubby worms had pushed open the flap and were feeling around inside.

"Hey pimple," growled a voice I recognized. "I brought you something from the dump. Hur hur hur."

I grimaced, knowing that I wasn't dreaming. The worms were fingers attached to Boris Hizzocks and pushing bits of rubbish, smelly horrible bits of icky food and rotting

stuff, into my nice clean hall.

I ran downstairs and trod on an orange peel smeared with ketchup. A stink of eggy fish ponged the air.

"Hey twinkletoes," snarled Boris Hizzocks. "Enjoy!" He kicked the door once for good measure, then stamped off down the path. I heard his nasty chortle, going "HUR HUR HUR" in the distance.

I heard the gate squeak. In a sudden fierce mood I scraped the icky glip off my slippers and opened the door.

What Happened Next

"Hey, Boris," I screamed, and he turned around, one hand still touching my gate. "Hey, Boris," I shouted, jabbing my finger in his direction. "Come back here! Now! And clean up this mess!"

Boris looked at me in disbelief and turned bright angry red. He made a growling sound. How hairy he is, I thought. How horrid. And his smell hadn't been improved much by the trip to the dump, either. He let go

of the gate and took a step towards me.

"THAT'S RIGHT," I roared, "COME AND CLEAN UP THIS MESS, YOU … STEWED PORRIDGE BRAIN!"

Boris stopped in mid-step and turned pale. With anger, I presumed.

"THAT'S RIGHT," I screamed, "I'M TALKING TO YOU!"

Unbelievably, he now took a step backwards. Equally unbelievably, I took a step forward. I zinged more insults at him, pressing home my advantage.

"MILKWIT!" I shouted. "POO-BREATH! APECURD-TWIZZLE-TROTTING-NINNYSKAT!"

I advanced and he backed away. It was as if I had been suddenly possessed by a demon of uncontrollable fury. He even started to look afraid. The truth was, I was a bit afraid myself. In fact, I was going berserk.

Berserking

Chapter seventeen of THE LOST SECRET ART OF KENJO by Granny Samurai deals with berserking. Berserking is the gift of uncontrollable fury emerging from the  inner core of your body. Granny Samurai is a natural berserker and so is the Monkey King. My Uncle Vesuvio is a natural opposite. He is a cool customer, as am I, or at least as I was, up until that moment.

Granny Samurai writes, *When you are afraid, your stomach feels sick. When you are angry, your face feels hot and your eyes and veins pop out. When you are on high alert, everything is sharp, including your ears. And when you are berserking, you are hot and cold and sharp and sick altogether. You BECOME your rage.*

I said, "You mean you go utterly and completely out of control?"

"A true berserker," said Granny Samurai, twiddling her little finger, "controls the uncontrollable."

"The Non-Silent Howl of Ultimate Destruction!" I said suddenly. "That's berserking!"

Granny nearly smiled. "Berserking for beginners," she replied tartly, and cracked her knuckles with a sound like popcorn popping. "But everybody starts somewhere."

Back to me, berserking.

I advanced down the garden path gibbering and howling with rage. My finger pointed straight at Boris and my eyes focused on his. Like a dog, he didn't like being stared at, and he continued to back away. Then his heel caught on a paving stone and he fell over.

"No!" he shouted.

"YES!" I shouted back, and reached out to grab him. A warning light went on in my brain. Berserking was all well and good, but Boris was still bigger and stronger than I. What would he do when I made contact? I needn't have worried.

"Heeelp!" he shouted in supreme terror, and his face changed colour for the third time.

Then something grabbed me instead.

"Muummmy!" screamed Boris, his face yellow as custard, and I would have screamed myself,

but a hard calloused
hand had clamped
itself over my mouth and
was hauling me swiftly upwards by the hair.

"Ummmmpfff," I squealed, through rough
and hairy fingers, "umpfff!" And the world
swung upside down as another hand seized
me by the foot and tossed me into the air like
a rag doll.

"Aarghhhh!" screamed Boris Hizzocks
beside me as the primals of the Monkey
King bore us up and away over the roof of 5
Summerhill Road, to whence I did not know.
So Boris hadn't been scared of me at all. He
had been scared of what he saw behind me.

As I have committed myself to scribing a true story, I will forcibly admit that this annoyed me more than a little.

A Short Montage of Current Events

This is us, being borne swiftly away through the treetops.

If you want to know what it felt like, simply imagine being pinched and pulled through a high hedge by a gang of evil flying dwarves while constantly thinking you will fall and strike the ground below.

This is Granny Samurai, opening her attic window and looking out and up, too late to save me – or Boris either if she could be bothered.

She was probably too distracted by the Friday Sports Round-Up.

"Thanks a lot!" I shouted.

And this is
Boris Hizzocks,
mouth agape
(which means
open like a drain),
eyes spinning,
processing with
feeble brainpower
what has just
happened to him.
Until his brain
overloads,
that is, and
shuts down.
The ground
beneath us zipped
past. I listened to the
primals' ghastly chitter.
Unlike Boris, I realized
exactly what had
happened.

Ignoring Granny Samurai's solemn warning about leaving the safety of the house, I had done just that. Outside, the Monkey King's servants had been waiting. Metaphysically speaking, their royal master had

reached out and closed his fist around me. *Dammit,* was the last thought issued by my brain before I, too, fainted.

A Note on Fainting

In my opinion, fainting, like sleeping, is a kind of time travel. Your brain shuts down and you awake, most alarmingly, in the future. What future would I awaken in? Luckily I had fainted so I wasn't able to worry about it.

The Future

I awoke from my faint and looked around. My face was scratched and my clothes were ripped and torn. Bits of leaves and twigs

stuck in my hair
and the world
was upside down.
With dawning
horror I realized
that in fact I was
upside down, tied
and gagged and
hanging from
my feet like a
bat in an attic
somewhere.
A very
small attic.
Beside me
Boris Hizzocks
had yet to resume consciousness (which was
fine by me), and outside I could hear faint
human voices getting fainter. A kind of pink
light filtered in from one side, and I turned
my head to perceive a grimy window.

"AAGGHHHH!" screamed a primal, pushing its ugly face against the glass on the other side and startling me with vigour. I looked away while it hooted with laughter. The pink light outside was cherry blossom. I suddenly knew exactly where I was.

It wasn't an attic.

In fact I am tied to the rafters of the pagoda on Japanese Island near the elephant gate within the town zoo. You can't see me because I am on the inside. I don't know why I'm here and I'm not even sure if I want to ponder it. Evening is descending and the visitors are streaming towards the exits. Some crisp bags swirl in their wake. On the signpost to the monkey house a pigeon with a baleful eye keeps solitary watch. Something tells me it is the

same one that

watched me

the last time. A horrible sense of Dijon vu starts prickling up and down my spine.

Dijon Vu

This is French and describes the prickly feeling you get when you know you've felt something before. Dijon is a famous mustard which causes head

prickle. "Vu" means seen. My brain had seen enough to know it needed to find a way out of there fast. I started struggling with the knots. I got nowhere.

"Samuel," said a voice behind me. "Is that you?"

I turned around and blinked. Since when did Boris Hizzocks call me Samuel? Normally he used a selection of much more viscous words. But Boris was still out cold. I blinked again and perceived behind him in the shadows a large pale snake's head floating

towards me.
It had tiny
pink eyes that
feasted on
mine and
a thin
flickery
tongue
that went
in and
out.

"It's me,
Samuel," said the
snake in a whispery
voice, and hissed, "your Uncle Vesuvio."

I blinked, unlike the snake, and peered again. I saw my uncle's head squeezing towards me through a loop of boa.

"Uncle Vesuvio!" I emitted in amazement, and the head did its best to nod. "What are you doing here?" With rising horror I saw that his previously distinguished grey hair had turned completely white. Then his mouth opened and he spoke in the whispery tones I had just heard.

"It's a trap, Samuel. You have to get out of here. Before the Monkey King arriv—"

The snake blinked and squeezed my uncle's voice shut. But I had heard enough. The Monkey King was on his way. Our doom was looming and it was up to me to do something to prevent it. But what?

Interesting Facts About Snakes That Squeeze

The boa constrictor is the second biggest squeezing snake in the world. It can squeeze the life out of a cow if it is large enough. (The boa, not the cow.) The biggest squeezer is the anaconda of Amazonian jungle fame.

"I knew her," said Granny Samurai when I mentioned this interesting fact later.

"Who?" I asked.

"Anna Conda," she replied. "She was the premier female wrestler of Amazonia. For a while, anyway," she cackled, and cracked her knuckles loudly.

"Anaconda is a snake," I corrected, "not a wrestler."

"She used to wrestle snakes," said Granny Samurai. "That's how she got her moniker. What a gal!"

DING DONG DING

In the meantime, however, I had no
premier snake wrestler to assist me – or
Granny Samurai for that matter. Instead
I writhed in the pagoda and tried to pull my
toes loose. To no avail. Although my hands
were free, my feet remained immutably
knotted to the wooden rafters. I jerked up and
down like a yo-yo, my lower digits throbbing
and glowing like fairy lights. The primals
had eaten my shoes and used my socks as
rope. I was irritated about the socks.
They were green with white mice
on them and quite humorous. My
uncle, who had guardianed me since
I was very small, had given them
to me once as a present. Now
he was tied up in a boa and
my socks were stretched and pulled beyond
repair. My feet, meanwhile, were moving into
volcanic itch territory. And where was my so-
called ally when I needed her?

Friday Sports Round-Up

At 4 Summerhill Road was the answer,
watching the sports channel at full blast on
her ninety-eight-inch flatscreen TV.

"TV help concentration," she said
when I challenged her about it later.
"Concentration = medication for
mistakes. Help brain plan big."

"Thank you," I said ironically.

"Don't mention it," she replied, somewhat menacingly. "Again."

This is Granny Samurai, "concentrating". As she concentrates she is polishing her wooden leg with beeswax. The leg is one of three she owns and is made of Madagascan rosewood, which is very hard and inlaid with cryptic runes whose top-secret meaning she will not reveal. Her Black Centurion double-action repeater is oiled and fully armed. She is always fully armed. When I asked her what the runes meant, she grunted, "Charms, for power and protection."

"You mean like spells?" I said politely, and thought, but didn't say, that Modern Science considers spells and charms to be for the simple-minded. Granny Samurai swivelled one eyeball and aimed it at me. "Pishposh," she snorted rudely. "Gibblegabble."

"Well maybe they work if you believe in them," I offered even more politely, slightly aghast as usual that she had seized upon my innermost thoughts.

"Hah," she snozzled with extreme unpoliteness. "You don't have to believe in proper spells for them to work. Proper spells work anyway. Basta!"

172

Tickle
Tickle
Tickle
CREAK

In the Absence of Spells

But as I didn't know any spells then anyway, and as my feet were expanding like balloons, the point was excessively moot, which means beside the point. Instead I opined that as my socks had been stretched a lot already, maybe I could stretch them even more. Hence, and in the absence of any better idea, I commenced jerking up and down like a bat whose feet have been glued

while my toes
screamed and the
primals hooted
and honked with
laughter at my
undignified
behaviour.
I ignored
their mocking,
however, as an
urgent departure
before the arrival
of the Monkey King seemed to me
to be priority 1A. I pulled and jerked and
got absolutely nowhere until a scrap of white
paper with a tiny number inscribed on it
fluttered out of my pocket. I grabbed it with
both hands and a spark of hope flared in my
breast. I didn't have a
mobile but I knew
somebody who did.

With my toes nearly breaking,
I pendulated back and forth until I could
reach Boris. I grabbed his hair with both
hands and held on. His eyes snapped open.

This is me, hanging by my toes, fingers
gripping Boris Hizzocks' hair.

His hair was sticky and thick, like him,
and I hoped I would be able to let go again
quickly.

"OWWW!" he roared, and started
thrashing about vigorously. "Leggo you
muppet."

A mobile slid out
of his pocket and
plummeted past
me to the ground.
Nooo…! I thought,
trying to catch it
with one hand. But
I needn't have worried.
The attentive reader
will recall that Boris
was famous for
"borrowing" other
people's phones.
A second one fell
past my nose,
and then a third.
That one I caught.
While Boris bellowed,
I swung away from him
and dialled the number
on the paper.

The phone rang. There was a click and a voice answered, "Who there?"

"Samuel," I replied.

"Never heard of him," said the voice. "Goodbye."

"Wait!" I screamed. "It's me, Sam. From next door. With the cake mix."

"Only joking," said the voice. "I know Sam. Point phone at primals please. Quick quick."

I believe it was the "please" that alarmed me most. Granny Samurai is not famous for frills of politesse. I glanced around. The primals were becoming agitated and pointing.

One gnashed its
teeth in my direction.
I held out the phone
and a voice came
through the speaker,
"*Sulimanasulimansalandra.*"
The primals blinked and
froze. Boris closed his eyes
and ceased his roaring. My
uncle closed his eyes also.
The boa stiffened,
then relaxed.
My socks ripped.
With a rending of
expensive threads,
I dropped head first
from the rafters to the
ground below. It will
suffice to close this
chapter by scribing
one word. *Ouch!*

"When the Bough Breaks"

This is a line from a poem I was forced to learn by heart in school. It went through my mind as I headed for the pagoda floor. Then it came out of my mouth as I landed. However, it would have been supremely ouchier if a pile of cherry blossoms blown in from the tree outside hadn't softened my landing. The pink petals puffed into the air around me and stuck to my perspiring forehead. I wiped them off and got them all over my fingers.

The mobile vanished
in the pile. I jumped to
my feet and my toes agonized. Then
my head agonized as a stunned primal
bounced off it, nearly knocking me down
again. A nanosecond later the rafters rained
primals, which didn't wake, even as they
thumped onto the ground around me.

"Quick Sam quick," said a voice from the
phone buried somewhere in the blossoms.

I grabbed the snake and started to
unwind my uncle. *Here we go round the
mulberry bush,* sang my brain while
I was doing it. At least I think it
was my brain.

Why Quote Poetry?

As a scribe I admire poems because they are a kind of shortcut to the intensity of the moment. They are prose boiled down to make it strong. Granny Samurai says poetry is stupid. Actually she says, "Pillypally poetry ping pal. Sillybilly rimrhymes. Pooh!"

Possibly she doesn't need poetry because she lives the intensity of the moment anyway.

Back to the Snake

I kept unwinding. Luckily my uncle was still breathing and I could see colour coming back into his face, though not his hair.

But dusk and the Monkey King were coming
also, and I wanted very much for us not to be
there when they arrived. The snake was dry
and smooth to touch, not slithery or cold like
I expected. It was like handling a leather belt.
Until it woke up that is.

Under my fingers the snake coiled and
its head turned and pinned me with an
unblinking hypnotic stare. A ripple of flexing

muscle went through its body and my uncle turned vivid red. I heard a cracking sound and hoped it wasn't one of his ribs.

"**SSSSSSSS**," went the snake, and its tongue hissed out at me like a flickering blue flame from a cigarette lighter. Without thinking, I did something  neither of us expected. I grabbed the tongue and squeezed.

Surprise Surprise

"Surprise Surprise" is chapter eighteen of

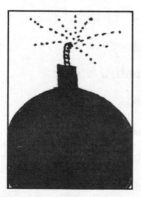

THE LOST SECRET ART OF KENJO by Granny Samurai. *The element of surprise,* writes Granny Samurai, *occurs when you surprise your opponent. ELEMENTAL surprise*

is when you surprise him most elementally. SUPPLEMENTAL elemental surprise is when you surprise yourself in the process. The careful reader will notice that all three kinds had just happened here.

A Tongue Twister

The snake blinked and tried to pull away. I dug my thumbnail into its tongue and held on.

"HZZZZZ," went the snake with irritability, and wriggled ripples up and down its body, vibrating my uncle into consciousness.

"Uncle," I called with extreme urgency. "Heeelp!" He looked at me groggily.

"Heeelp!" I called again, and the snake wrapped its tail around my bare ankle and started pulling. I squeezed harder. The tongue felt like a fillet of anchovy under my nail. The snake's eyes bulged and, with a viscous twist, it suddenly released my uncle from its squeezing embrace and tumbled him dizzily to the ground. Then it unhinged its jaw (this is how boas are able to eat cows, etc) and prepared to swallow my arm. I cringed, then suddenly my uncle's hand reached up and chopped the boa on the neck. It collapsed like a piece of string and I collapsed with it.

"Chop chop long last," cackled
a voice behind us, and I turned and
gaped. Standing in the pagoda
doorway, Granny Samurai was
grinning in our direction. The
thinnest mobile phone I had ever
seen pulsed greenly in her hand
and gave her face a goblin glow.

HOP! HOP!

"Penalty shootout," she said. "Sorry I took so long." Then she dropped the phone into her bag and unstrapped her wooden leg. Hopping lightly over the knocked-out primals she bashed the stirring snake hard with it, on the conker. "To be sure to be sure," she said, and grinned. "Game nearly over," she added. "Let's go."

POFF!

The Application of Learning

The attentive reader will recall chapter four of THE LOST SECRET ART OF KENJO, which touches briefly on bashing on the conker. *A Madagascan rosewood leg is seriously*  *effective,* Granny Samurai writes, *but a golf club will do also. Be flexible.*

Returning to Leaving

Obeying Granny Samurai's command to leave, I turned with automism to go. Possibly I was used to it by now as, after all, she had been giving me orders all week. Though I was also happy to leave, not forgetting the nerve-wracking imminence of the Monkey King. But then my uncle spoke up with sudden authorial firmness.

"Samuel, stop. Henrietta, this is not a

game." Granny Samurai swivelled her dark eyes and squinted the pupils at him.

"*Sulimanasulimansalandra,*" she whispered, and made a forking gesture with two fingers in his direction. My uncle held up his palm and there was a sizzling sound like an egg being dropped in a hot pan.

"Don't be silly, Henrietta," he said, and grabbed my arm.

"Silly self," she muttered and seized my other arm. "Come on Sam. Let's go."

My uncle tightened his grip. "No, Sam," he said, then added, "Henrietta, this is far too dangerous for Samuel."

"Wait," I said, with great and growing puzzlement. "You mean, you *know* each other?" They both ignored me completely.

"Sam fine. Help big," snapped Granny to my uncle, who frowned and told her to stay out of his business, please. "Too late," she snozzled as I tried once again to intersect between them.

"Excuse me," I repeated, and both turned around to shush me. Successfully irritated, I reached up and applied the only thing I had truly learnt thus far. I ear-pinched them both. "Now!" I said. "Now you have to listen to me!" Big mistake bonanza!

The Monkey King Arrives

One nanosecond later and my eardrums were assaulted by a roar of savage mutation.

The air filled with sticky monkey spit. Outside the pagoda a binormous (enormous x 2) crimson-haired fury landed in the cherry tree, bending it almost to the ground with a massive savage creak. Japanese Island shook and the wall of the pagoda blew off into the evening sky. Twigs and cherry blossoms pelted down around me and a great pungent pong filled my nose and lungs. The Monkey King had arrived and was excessively vexated. Worse than that, I had temporarily decommissioned my only two allies.

VOOM! is the sound the Monkey King's hand makes as he sweeps me to one side and sends me tumbling across the perfectly raked gravel of the Zen Garden outside. His trap is sprung. He doesn't need me as bait any more.

VOPP! is the sound the Monkey King's fists make as he grabs Granny Samurai and Uncle Vesuvio and bonks their heads together. Hard! Her wooden leg clatters to the ground.

"GOOOARRRAAHHH!"
This is the scream the
Monkey King issues forth as
he flexes his toes and flings
himself into the sky like a
departing hairy Boeing 747.
He has my uncle in one
hand and Granny Samurai
in the other.

"Stop," I wheezed weakly, shaking gravel from my ears, and a small faint voice, most probably not my conscience, spoke in my brain. "Quick quick Samuel Johnson. Act not think. Now!"

Departing Japanese Island

I acted by grabbing the cherry tree. The immense saturating weight of the Monkey King had bent it to the ground like a bow. My fingers closed around a branch tip just as he flung himself howling skywards. A second later the tree snapped back into position and hurled me after him.

Here's me, flying through the air.
As you can see, I am not in exact
one hundred per cent control
of my flight plan. There's the
Monkey King up ahead, his
hair blown back by the
screaming vortex. I am
screaming also. Behind
me you can see the
pagoda, or what
remains
of it.

And underneath us is the zoo.
The wind blows my scream away
as I come in for a crash landing.

The Lion's Den

BOOM!

and

OUCH!

Touchdown! In front
of me the Monkey
King had already
landed, my uncle and
a groggy Granny still
gripped tightly in his
fists. In the same
second of ultimate
impact he flung
himself forward again, his hind legs ripping
a hole in the fence around the top of the lions'
enclosure. By now it was dusk, and the large
yellow beasts blinked as he appeared and
disappeared under their noses. I know this

because I landed among them two seconds later. Except I didn't rebound or do the disappearing part afterwards. Instead, I lay on the sandy ground and wondered if I had broken any bones, and if so, how many. The lions started dribbling and drawing closer. One licked its lips with a tongue like a big red sock. I was entirely trapped.

OOFF!

Some Lion Facts

Lions are the largest predatorial cats in the universe and hunt at night. As twilight was now gathering this explains the licking of the lips in anticipatory relish. Also lions are eaters of carrion (which means dead meat), though if the meat is still alive, they are quite happy to kill it first.

Famous lions in history include the lion of Androcles, who was Greek (Androcles, not the lion) and had a thorn in its paw that was hurting until Androcles pulled it out and they became friends.

But that was only one lion and possibly not a
meat-eater, either, on account of its whinging
over a thorn.

Now I was surrounded by a pride of lions,
all of which feasted on meat. I knew this
because when the biggest one roared in my
face I could see shards of bone and old
mealtimes on his fangs and smell
his terrifically bad breath.

I raised myself up on one elbow
and considered making a run for the moat
around the enclosure. *Ha ha ha,* said my brain
in high amusement. *Good luck with that.* The
lions drew closer. There was no doubt about it.
I was in a serious emergency.

Emergencies

Chapter thirty of THE
LOST SECRET ART OF
KENJO by Granny Samurai
is called "Emerging
Emergencies: What to Do
When You Don't Know What to Do". There
is a blank space after it.

"Fill in self," shrugs Granny Samurai.
"Everybody's emergency different."

"Well what would you have done about
the lions?" I asked later.

"Not what you did," she chortled, and her
false teeth rattled in her head.

"I did my best under the circumstances,"
I said stiffly, my uncle's voice emerging
from my mouth.

"Hee hee hee," wheezed Granny.
"You betcha."

In fact, building on my success with
the snake, what I had done was grab the

biggest lion by the whiskers and hold on tight.

"Gooooaaaar!" it said, and unlike the snake, raised a vast clawed paw to smite me.

I hadn't thought of that, I thought, and braced myself for instant doom.

Saved by a Summons

Then a strange noise sounded over the zoo and the lion froze in mid-swipe. The noise sounded like a giant wasp blowing on a vuvuzela. It penetrated my skull and drilled into my two fillings. As if I had suddenly ceased to exist, the lion turned its head and listened. Then, followed by the others, it padded over to the moat and jumped lightly across. They headed towards the source of the noise.

Deafened and weirded out,
I abandoned calmness and followed
them out of the enclosure. The noise sounded
again. From all over the zoo exotic animals
were moving silently towards its source.
Across the way, a hippo clambered into his
moat and made a bridge for the others. A
camel swayed past me, followed by a skunk,
and a hedgehog. I realized it wasn't just the

exotic animals that were on the move, it was *all* animals. Suddenly it seemed that the whole world around me was wriggling and writhing and rustling. I saw foxes and rats, birds and squirrels, hedgehogs, warthogs and lizards. Something slithered over my bare feet and I looked down. The ground around my toes was a river of insects, worms and frogs. I closed my eyes and suppressed a scream of high-pitched panic. Then a wet something or other slithered quickly around my ankles and my head went dizzy. It was an eel and I hoped it wasn't electric. An elephant pounded past and smaller animals on the ground, including me, moved quickly aside to make patches for it to walk in. Against my will, I found myself being swept along by the animalistic tide.

The Lair of the Monkey King

Now the noise grew even louder as we approached its source. The buzzing throb punished my ears and exacerbated my brain greatly. The skin on my scalp tightened, forcing my hairs to stand up very straight.

We were nearing the middle of the zoo and the animals were slowing down. The buzzing was immense. There, in front of us, at the exact zoo's heart, was a huge old monkey puzzle tree, a gift from New Zealand, which has many of the trees but no monkeys to puzzle them with.

And high in its spiky green branches, toes and fingers gripping firmly, the Monkey King had spread himself lavishly and was blowing with full primal fury into what looked like a brightly painted conch shell. That was the WOOWOOWOOO noise I had been hearing. Beneath him on the branch, tied in a vine of a thousand knots, Granny Samurai and Uncle Vesuvio swung like two giant piñatas, which is Mexican for something you hang and hit. The Monkey King held up his red-tipped claws for silence, and there was silence.

The Calm Before the Storm

"AUURRAOOOW," he shouted, holding up Granny Samurai's handbag and shaking it vigorously. The animals listened but didn't say anything.

210

"HAABBA MABBA MOO HAA AAHH," roared the Monkey King. The animals, even the creepiest of crawlies, were totally still. "OOOMA OMA GRANNY OOOBA," screamed the orator, and opened the bag whilst watched by a million eyes. "HEEEBA," he yowled and stuck his hand inside. "AAHHHHHH!" he screamed, with thrice the volume of his previous intensity, as a giant Warsupial rat snapper closed with vigorousness on his fingers. It turns out that Granny Samurai always keeps one in her bag to deter pickpockets, though who in their right mind would want to pickpocket Granny Samurai I don't know. The sobering fact is that it would be considerably safer to punch an African bull rhino in the ear after he has received irritating news than to pickpocket Granny Samurai.

The Monkey King glared at his bleeding fingers, then bit the trap off and crunched it up with his gold teeth. I felt quite faint at that, and tried to make myself small. I didn't want to imagine what he would do if he noticed me amongst the hedgehogs.

Then a voice hissed in my ear. "Don't turn around," it said.

I turned around.

Don't Think of a Wazzymoogle

Chapter twenty-eight of THE LOST SECRET ART OF KENJO by Granny Samurai deals with making people do things. Granny Samurai writes, *Don't think of a wazzymoogle, bibbers*

the poet, and thus you think of a wazzymoogle.

"What poet?" I asked.

"Any stupid poet," she said. "Who cares! The point is if you want somebody to do something, just tell them not to do it."

"Rubbish," I said.

"You left the house," she pointed out, "when I told you not to."

"That was different," I replied.

"No it wasn't," she said, and I demurred.

"Don't turn round," said the voice now behind me in the zoo, and I immediately did. There, ugly as a wart, stood Boris Hizzocks, grinning.

In both hands he held Granny Samurai's
Madagascan rosewood appendage. I braced
for terror and emergency. But then he spoke.

"Don't worry, Samuel," he said calmly.
"Things are not as they seem."

Why Things Are Not As They Seem

This is a philosophical enquiry and the answer
is that things are never as they seem because
if they were we would always know exactly
what was going on. And of course we don't.
My Uncle Vesuvio says that philosophy is the
minor science of making up hard answers
that don't help, to easy questions that don't
matter. Do we exist? is a major example. The
answer is yes because if we didn't, we wouldn't
be able to ask the question to begin with. I am
not going to be a philosopher when I grow up.
I am too pithy and there is even less money
in it than poetry.

Back to Terror and Emergency

And Boris Hizzocks didn't clonk me. Instead, he reached out and patted me on the cheek. "All things going plan plan," he whispered, then clacked his teeth with odd familiarity.

"Granny Samurai?" I said, unnerved. For a weird and confusing second I caught a glimpse of somebody else staring at me through Boris's eyes: someone small and dark and dangerous. It was like a person appearing at a window in an otherwise deserted house. "Granny Samurai," I whispered. "Is that you?"

"Megawocka," said Boris, and winked.

A roar brought
me back to my
surroundings. High up
in the tree the Monkey King had closed his
hands around the second line of Granny
Samurai's ultimate pickpocket defence,
i.e. one stuffed Tobogian nettlefish.

"ARRAAGGHH!"

he screamed, and
with a movement
too quick
to follow,
shredded the
bag to pieces
with his long
curved nails.
Its contents
exploded into the air
with abundance.

"That was a Prada bag, you pigglepoggle
monkey nutter," muttered
Boris behind me. "I'm not
happy about that."

But the Monkey
King just grinned.
It seemed he had
finally got what he
wanted. With a flick

of his hairy wrist
he reached out and
caught something falling
through the air. Then he held it
up. It was long and thin and looked
like a badminton racquet made of wicker,
only without strings. The last time I had seen
it, it had been hanging on my uncle's wall of
ultimate mementoes. Not any more!

With a long
triumphal
hoot the
Monkey King
brandished
it like a
microphone
and screamed through it.
"OOOLAOOLAOOOH!"

An instant answering cry went
up from the animals around.

"HOOOPLA!" they roared.

"OOLAOOLAOOOHAAA!"
bellowed the Monkey King, twice as loud.
  "BAAAAAAH!" the animal
kingdom screamed in response, and the
worms beneath my feet wriggled in ecstatic
fevers. I wriggled too, I must report, most
jitteringly, for where before I had heard just
monkey noise, I now understood
everything the Monkey King was
saying. And it wasn't pretty.

"THE NON-ANIMALS ARE
TRICKY," he spake. "THE NON-ANIMALS
ARE MANY. MANY MANY TRICKS UP
MANY MANY SLEEVES. BUSY BUSY
BRAINS, THE NON-ANIMALS. THE
NON-ANIMALS MAKE OUCHY."

He twisted
his back and
wriggled his
shoulder
blades
where the
blue and
yellow
thing I had
noticed
before
seemed
stuck.

"THE NON-ANIMALS MAKE ALWAYS OUCHY! OUCHY YOU AND OUCHY ME. OUCHY US!" he screamed. "OUCHY OUCHY OUCHY!"

As you can see, Granny Samurai wasn't the only one with an excessively compact way of speaking. The Monkey King continued.

"THE NON-ANIMALS SQUEEZE US TOGETHER. SQUEEZE SQUEEZE NO AIR. SQUEEZE SQUEEZE NO WATER. SQUEEZE SQUEEZE NO FOREST. THE NON-ANIMALS LIVE IN BOXES. NO HAIR. WEAR CLOTHES. NO NAILS, MAKE NAILS. THE NON-ANIMALS TAKE THE ANIMALS AND PUT THEM IN ZOOS. TOO MUCH. NO MORE. STOP. STOP NOW. STOP OUCHY! STOP!"

"I'll show you ouchy, you monkey nutter," muttered Boris Hizzocks behind me. And with a shock, I realized who the non-animals

222

were. They were *us*. The Monkey King was talking about human beings, and he didn't much like us, either.

Certainly with Boris Hizzocks, he had a point.

"HERE TWO," screamed the Monkey King, and stamped on the branch beneath him. My Uncle Vesuvio opened his eyes groggily and looked at me. Granny Samurai still seemed to be out cold.

"THERE TWO TOO," screamed the Monkey King, and pointed right at me and Boris. Then, in a gesture I had seen before, he shaped his pointing claw like a cobra and folded his left foot behind like a scorpion's pincer. Around us, the animals moved away quickly. Like me, they knew what was coming next.

"Uh-oh," whispered Boris. "Brace brace."

But I had a better idea.

"Wait!" I shouted. "Before you annihilate us with a Non-Silent Scream of Ultimate Fury, what do you want? Your Hairy Highness," I added politely, recalling what my uncle says about good manners being the cornerstone of civilization.

"Don't think, stupid, act," whispered Boris behind me.

But I had tried *that* already and look where I had ended up. "Would you mind shutting up?" I said savagely, forgetting my uncle's good-manners advice for a second. "I'm trying to save our lives!"

Boris rolled his eyes and snorted, but he shut up all the same.

225

The Monkey King examined me with fierce eyes, but paused.

"You told me you wanted to negotiate," I pleaded, "that day at my door. At least, your servants did," I amended.

The Monkey King hesitated, just for a second, and I could see him remembering. Then his face hardened and I could see him deciding ... against us.

But that one second was enough.

In that
one second
the knots fell
off Granny
Samurai like
Houdini,
the escapist
of old.
In that
one second
she gripped the
Monkey King's foot with her
now free hand and swung herself up behind
him. In that one second she blasted him with
a Ting-Tong punch that launched him high
into the dark night sky; and as he launched,
she plucked, with a movement of supreme
delicacy, the racquet thingy from his grasp,
then slashed her diamond hook to snatch
his brightly coloured conch from his other
hand. Finally, grabbing the topmost

branch with all six toes, she opened her mouth and howled at the rising moon with a noise like a giant kettle coming to the boil. YES! I thought,
and was

about to punch the air in triumph when an awkward thought occurred to me.

If Granny was no longer Boris, who was? I was about to find out.

Where's Boris?

"Hey maggot
breath," said a
voice I knew,
in bullying tones.
"Hur hur hur." And
a hard hand grabbed
my shoulder from behind. "What are
you doing here, *pimple*?"

I turned to face my enemy
the first, and true to form,
he drew back his fist to
punch me. Then the
Monkey King fell
out of the sky and
squashed him flat
as a pair of ironed
underpants.

230

Boris nil.

Monkey King also nil.

Granny Samurai: game, set and match!

Nearly

Here's me, surrounded by animals of all
shapes and sizes. There's Boris Hizzocks,
squashed mightily under the Monkey
King. There's my Uncle
Vesuvio, struggling out of his
knots, and there's Granny
Samurai, about to make
a speech through the
racquet thingy.
The animals are
watching and
listening.

"Go back to your homes," she said loudly. "Go back to your burrows, your holes, your caves, your nests and your roosts. And go in peace. Or else," she added, with sinister intent. Nothing moved. "I mean it," she said, and a parrot somewhere repeated mockingly, "I mean it. I mean it!" Granny Samurai clacked her teeth and spat on the ground below the branch. One hand shifted to her Black Centurion double-action repeater. "I'm still upset about the bag," she said.

A Tense Moment

Chapter thirty-one of THE LOST SECRET ART OF KENJO by Granny Samurai deals with tense moments.

Tense moments, she writes, *are characterized by palpitations, sweating and a dry mouth. Enjoy!*

"What do you mean, enjoy?" I asked.

"Have fun while happening," she answered.

I expressed with some exasperation that I knew what the word *enjoy* meant.

"So why ask stupid question?" she retorted rhetorically.

"I mean, how can you enjoy palpitations, sweating and a dry mouth?" I persisted.

"Because I am an adrenalin addict," she said.

"Why you think I drink so much coffee? Hee hee hee." She gave a laugh like somebody stabbing a bagpipe to death.

Back to the Real-life Tense Moment

She wasn't laughing now. But neither was she doing much palpitating, either. Like an ancient carved goddess glowering down from the branch of her tree, she stared down the animals and the tension tensed.

It was my uncle who broke the uncomfortable silence, but then as a diplomat that's his job.

"Henrietta," he said, "we need to talk."

"Talk!" screamed the parrot sarcastically, and in a movement too quick to follow, something flew from Granny Samurai's hand and there was a loud squawk, then silence. The silence was filled by an ominous rumble. The animals hadn't liked that. Beside me the Monkey King stirred.

"Ahem," I spake nervously, "Uncle Vesuvio, I think the Monkey King is waking up."

"Just clonk his nut Sam," said Granny irritably. "You may use my leg."

"No clonking, Samuel, please," said my uncle, which was substantially preferable. I had seen the Monkey King in action and would rather clonk a ticking bomb.

"OK, I'll clonk," said Granny, and stuffing the racquet thingy into her belt, she hopped quickly from her branch. One millisecond too late. The Monkey King was only pretending.

With a roar of a thousand irritations he jumped up and snapped his fists together into a Hammer of Sensational Vortex and plunged them at Granny. She ducked and sliced at his solar plexus with a stick produced from somewhere on her person.

He sucked
his stomach in
and kicked at the air where she
had just been. She whirled her stick and flew
like a helicopter over his head, landing with
a roar and swiping at his clenched feet. He
jumped like, well, a monkey, and she sliced a
divot from the ground that a golfer wielding
a bulldozer would have been proud of.

The animals moved back but kept watching.
The fighting increased.

Now the Monkey
King pointed a red-tipped
claw at Granny and blasted
her with a Howl of Deep Sonic Sundering.
With a twisting wrist movement she
deflected the outrage and the monkey
puzzle behind her
shivered and
divested half
its foliage.

She lashed out with her stick, and a branch above the Monkey King exploded with a crack and toppled towards him. He howled and caught it, thrusting the broken pointy end straight at her.

"SHISHKABOB!" he screamed, or something like it, which made much more

sense in the context. But Granny Samurai
stamped her leg into the ground
and, pushing off mightily
with her stick, started

spinning like a tornado while the branch
was ground to powder like a toothpick
being pushed into a buzz saw. A nearby
porcupine was showered with
sawdust and backed up quickly,
sneezing. The climax
hurtled towards us.
At least, I thought it
was the climax.

Then a big hand grabbed me again. I looked around and Boris Hizzocks was leering at my visage with his fist drawn back, taking up where he'd left off.

Apparently he hadn't been flattened enough.

"I know I'm just dreaming," he smirked, "but I'm still going to enjoy this." And he unleashed the punch.

What a muppet, I thought, as his fist rocketed towards me. What a crumpet. Doesn't he have anything better to do in his miserable life than bully me, for NO REASON AT ALL?

Outrage swelled in my breast. Before the

unleashed fist squashed my nose, I reached
out and pushed the puncher, not hard but just
hard enough.

"Softly softly," said Granny, grinning,
when I reported later what I had done.
"Always just enough, never too much."
Which was maybe wise but a bit rich coming
from her.

Boris looked at me in confusion. The
little push had nudged him off balance. His
fist whisked the air a mere 1.2 cm in front of
my nose, then he toppled slowly backwards,
right onto the sneezing porcupine, which
was scurrying away from the turbulence of
the Monkey King and Granny Samurai's
titanic battle.

"Ouch," said Boris,
looking surprised.

PUSH!

WHISK!

Interesting Facts About Porcupines

Porcupines can grow to the size of a large dog and are covered in spikes called quills. This is fact number one. Fact number two is that all quills point in one direction, which is backwards, away from the porcupine's head. This means that the porcupine can't go backwards, only forwards, as Boris was about to find out.

And fact number three is that porcupine quills have tiny little barbs in them, like mini fish-hooks, which keep them ultra-attached to what- or whomsoever they are plunged into. This is excessively painful and to be avoided considerably at all costs.

"OUCH!" screamed Boris at louder volume. The porcupine tried turning to see what had got stuck to him. "OUUUUCH!" howled Boris with even greater than louder volume. I believe this was the point at which he realized that he was not actually dreaming. Then a snake trying to escape the battle slithered up his trousers and disappeared. This confirmed his realization. Boris stiffened and went green. His scream turned off like a tap.

dat's mah brudder

Behind us the great battle continued. Now Granny Samurai and the Monkey King were duelling with special weapons.

The Application of Special Weapons

Chapter forty-five of THE LOST SECRET ART OF KENJO deals with the use of special weapons. *Keep them Top Secret,* writes Granny Samurai. *Forget you even have them.*

"Why?" I asked.

"Because what is more secret than something you have forgotten?" she said.

"But if you forget them," I said, "what use are they?"

"None," she replied, "which is why you have to buy my book and learn all the other things instead."

I blinked and looked again. I realized

that Granny Samurai
and the Monkey King
were wielding vast
powerful weapons
that were ponderous
and totally invisible. All
I could see was the damage they left behind.
In slow motion, it seemed, she lifted a club
over her head. Then she jerked it forward.
In equally slow motion the Monkey King
blocked the blow and the air wobbled as
if something massive had shivered into a
thousand pieces. I felt my insides vibrate
as a wave of
sound and
fury passed
through
them.

Behind me, a hippo quivered
and toppled to the ground. *Ouch!* it
said in a surprisingly squeaky voice.

Above my head, a great invisible chain
with a massive weight attached sloughed past.
The Monkey King was swinging it towards
his foe. It struck and something sparked near
Granny Samurai's middle as she jumped back
quickly. The Monkey King advanced and the
trunk of the monkey puzzle splintered
as if chopped by
a giant hand.

The racquet thingy landed on the ground in front of me. The Monkey King's weapon must have snatched it from Granny's belt. I picked it up and looked at it curiously. It seemed to hum in my hand, sending quivers towards my elbow. I held it up to my mouth and shouted, "STOP!"

The fighting duo ignored me but all the other animals turned and looked in my direction.

"Samuel," screamed my uncle, "watch out!" I ignored him and tried again with another word that I had recently learnt. "SULIMANASULIMANSALANDRA!"

And everything stopped. Instantly!

"That's the thing about real spells," spoke a small dark voice in my mind. "Real spells work. It's got nothing to do with whether you believe in them or not." Then another voice spoke in my head, closer this time.

"Hurry," said my Uncle Vesuvio. "Hurry, nephew!" He was lying beside me on the ground, stretched out as if frozen in the act of diving. "Samuel, watch out!" he had screamed, and with a shock I saw he had been diving to save my life.

An invisible weapon had been coming right at me. I could see it clearly now. I had spoken the spell at just the right second.

"Hurry," called my uncle again, through frozen lips, "no time." I realized that the spell, though powerful, was only temporary. Soon the mills of time would grind on again. I had to do something quickly, and for once I knew exactly what to do. Whether it was the right thing or not, I would find out afterwards. I girded my lions and stepped forth.

254

How It Was I Knew What to Do

As a scribe I am a very large fan of reading, which leads to knowledge. Sometimes this knowledge is up front, like in *How to Build a Rocket,* and sometimes it is disguised, like in Aesop's Feebles. Feebles are simple stories told as a way of giving sideways advice. One of Aesop's greatest hits was about a Greek called Androcles (see chapter on lions) who pulled a thorn from a lion's paw. The thorn-pulling soothed the lion's blood-lust and later on they became good friends. I thought of this now, stepping forth with a bright idea to bring the battle to a savoury end. It was also my only idea. The Monkey King had an ouchy. I knew where it was. I intended ministering to him.

I Act

Heart palpitating, I approached where the Monkey King was crouched, frozen like the others, in mid-strike. His spiky hair blazed in all directions. His eyes were furious and flecked with gold.

"Hurry," said my uncle's voice again in my mind. I hurried.

Around me I could feel time building up as though against a giant dam, ready to cascade forth. I held my breath and climbed His Simian Highness. There, stuck between his shoulder blades, was what I sought. It was a thorn, sort of, and the skin around it was puckered and angry. I grabbed it with both hands and pulled. There was a sound like a sigh and a Pffffffff! In the same millisecond the dam broke, and time engulfed us again. The world restarted. Something invisible swished over my head and evaporated in the air. My uncle thumped to the ground. Granny Samurai landed on all threes near her wooden leg. And Boris Hizzocks resumed being dragged past by a confused porcupine whilst

258

howling (Boris, not the porcupine).

I looked at the thorn. It was blue with a yellow tip and more like a dart, really. I looked at the Monkey King. He was red and getting redder. Teeth spinning like a liquidizer, he turned to gibber at me, reaching out his arms while his fingers extended and flexed. My bowels went icy. With a deep-freeze shudder I suddenly remembered that Aesop-of-the-feebles-fame's life had ended when he was escorted off a cliff by his ancient Grecian public. They hadn't thought very much of his advice. I was starting to see why.

All's Well That Ends Well

"That was sneaky," said Granny Samurai, springing to my side with a sudden mighty leap. Her wooden leg was on again and I caught a quick glimpse of a spring retreating into it.

"Well done, nephew," said my Uncle Vesuvio, standing up and brushing himself off.

I stared at them in amazement. The Monkey King was about to grab me and they were calming down. Then I understood. For all his gibbering and liquidizing, the Monkey King was getting smaller and smaller. It was like watching the air leaving a balloon. His skin became wrinkly and saggy and he turned a deeper and deeper shade of red.

"NOOOOO," he wheezed with shrill
vocals and mouth wide open, showing his
tonsils vibrating in squeaky anger. "Nooooo," he
squealed again as his arms got shorter and
thinner and weaker. Now he was as small
as Granny Samurai and still shrinking.

And under my feet the ground
writhed as the worms corkscrewed
back into the earth. The insects fled,
and one by one the larger animals
moved away also. The lions went
back to their lair, the hippos clambered back
through their moats, the tapirs went back
to wherever they lived, too. Within minutes
there were only the non-animals left, all four
of us, and a shrinking Monkey King now
hardly bigger than a cat and dwindling fast.

"Isn't he going to stop?" I asked worriedly.

"Stop," hissed Granny Samurai, and he
stopped. He was now about as big as a chicken
and just as harmless, though still furious.

My uncle reached into his pocket and
pulled out a strange leather pouch with
special stitching. He held it open and a
sucking sound came out, pulling the
Monkey King inside.

My uncle closed the bag and knotted it.

"I'll take that Vesuvio," said Granny
Samurai, holding out
her hand. But my
uncle just frowned.

"Absolutely
not, Henrietta," he
replied, and you
could tell he really
meant it.

"Is your name really Henrietta?" I asked, grinning.

"Shut it," said Granny Samurai, glaring at me.

"Henny for short," said my uncle and grinned also. "But she doesn't like being called that."

"Better than being named after volcano," snapped Granny, and stamped her wooden peg into the earth. Around us, the destruction was immense.

"Monkey King caught now," she said thoughtfully. "Safe safe once more."

"Indeed," said my uncle. "No thanks to you."

"You're welcome," snorted Granny, and her face split open in a ferocious grin. "I enjoyed that," she added.

There Isn't Much More to Scribe

We took a taxi home and it was the same one that we had taken before. This time it cost seven pounds. The taxi was another strange coincidence, I thought, although chapter forty-seven of THE LOST SECRET ART OF KENJO states that there is no such thing as coincidence. That's all it states. It is the second pithiest chapter in the book.

The Ride Home

On the way home
I must have slept, and
at some point Uncle
Vesuvio carried me up
to bed and tucked me
in. That was Sunday
or Saturday, I was no
longer sure. Somewhere
along the way I had
lost nearly a whole
day, which was
still better
than Pope
Gregory, who
lost nearly a
fortnight back
in 1582. I had
no dreams

that night either, which was one
hundred per cent fine by me.

And Finally

In fact it was Sunday. *Sunday dawned bright and cheerful.*
This was a sentence I scribed
in my diary when
I woke up, hoping
it would be true.
And it was.

I went downstairs.
My uncle was in the kitchen
making apple pancakes,
which is the second best breakfast in the world.
(The best is chocolate pancakes.)

Outside, nothing
was happening.
Sundays, as I have
previously intoned,
are the second best
day of the weekend,
though sometimes boring.
But I am a person who can easily

occupy themselves and so I am never bored.
Plus I had seen enough interesting things over
the last week to scribe a book about them, if
I had nothing better to do.

"Sit down, Samuel," said my uncle, and
flipped a pancake onto my plate.
He is excessively dextrous at
certain things.

"I feel I owe you an explanation,"
he added.

"I think so," I agreed.
My uncle sipped his
Blue Mountain brew, which
is a world-famous coffee
and not instant. He
didn't squish it around
his teeth, either.

"Where is Granny Samurai?" I asked.

"She'll show up soon enough," said my uncle, "but in the meantime…" He started to explain.

The Great Explanation

The Monkey King is not a king like kings in the non-animal world. In the non-animal world, royalty pass on the crown to their children, even if their children are mad or weird or bald or good, which latter extremity is mostly not the case (see history).

The children of royalty then inherit thrones and jewels and other great sources of wealth, which is why they are called royalty from "royalties", which is money that dribbles into their coffers.

The Monkey King, however, is an honorary title bestowed, which means given, to a chosen monkey once every century. His job is to see how things are going in the animal world, which is not very well at the moment. And so he got angry and devised a great plan.

"You mean," I interrupted my uncle, "he decided to attack the non-animals?"

"No," he said, "he decided to try talking first, and see if he could reason with them. But negotiations went nowhere and then a certain person hit him with a dart to try to capture him.

PUFF!

That didn't work either. In fact, it enraged him. The rage caused him to swell and become more powerful."

"Monkey King in rage any old how," said a voice I knew, behind me. "Monkey King multo bonkers bad news bonanza. Monkey King long gone mad." And Granny Samurai plonked down loudly in a seat beside us.

"Perhaps," replied my uncle thoughtfully. "Perhaps." He paused and Granny Samurai helped herself to some coffee. My uncle continued. "In any case, the Monkey King had grown impatient with negotiation. So he kidnapped the negotiator."

"You?" I gasped.

"Indeed," replied my uncle.

Granny Samurai snorted. "Monkey King have summons singer already. Very dangerous. Wanted other thing too."

I frowned. "The summons singer?"

"The conch shell," answered my uncle, "for calling the animals. It is his Orb of Magisterial Office. His sceptre is—"

"The racquet thingy!" I interjected, with sudden lurid insight.

"The Inter-Species Communicator," corrected my uncle. "For talking to other animals. It was top, top, top secret and in my personal safekeeping. It was to be kept away from the Monkey King at all costs." Granny Samurai laughed and wagged a finger at him.

"Tricky Vesuvio," she cackled. "Hide in

study whole time. But Granny found it. Yes she did. Hee hee hee." She stuck the finger into her coffee and stirred with it.

"You mean the *Monkey King* found it," I amended accurately, "when he entered my dream and led you to it."

"Ahem," muttered Granny Samurai. "Shut it Sam pronto OK." She slurped her coffee loudly and did her best to look innocent.

Uncle Vesuvio turned pale and stared at her. "You involved Samuel in this, Henrietta?" he said incredulously. "After I specifically forbade it?"

"Sam not stupid," snapped Granny Samurai. "And you in Azerbaijan, NOT! Big ha ha!" My uncle eyeballed her coldly.

"I ask you to keep an eye on Samuel while I am engaged in a highly classified negotiation and—"

"Sam still here," interrupted Granny. "Limbs intact. Hair intact. All fingers and teeth present. Where problem? Oh, and thank you Granny for saving my life," she added piously. "You're welcome, V. Any time."

"Wait," I said, and looked at Granny Samurai. "You mean *you* were sending me those postcards?"

"*He* wrote them," she defended, pointing at my uncle. "Except last one," she added. "Granny wrote that." Then she opened her palms to show her empty hands. "Out of postcards," she said. "Out of time. Must act."

"Just *not*," said my uncle heavily, "by using Samuel as bait."

"To catch tiger get goat," snapped Granny. "Goat did well. Well done Sam. Will teach you more tricks."

"You will not,"
said my uncle angrily.

"Will so," snapped
Granny.

"STOP!"
I shouted.
They stopped.

"What about Boris Hizzocks?" I asked. "What was his role in all this?"

"Who?" said my uncle, having missed a considerable amount while he was not in Azerbaijan.

"School bully boy," said Granny Samurai. "*Boris hairius horribilus*. Pain pain for Samuel. OK now."

"I shall talk to the headmaster about him first thing tomorrow," said my uncle stiffly. "Don't worry, Samuel. I will take care of that."

"Er," said Granny Samurai, "maybe I should come with you."

"Absolutely not," said my uncle.

"Absolutely yes," said Granny.

"Not," said my uncle.

"Yes," said Granny.

"Stop!" I shouted again. "What I meant was, how were you Boris and he you, and where is he now?"

Granny Samurai looked at me and her

eyes were like darkest treacle. "Did soul swap quick quick, good for ten minutes. To sneak up on Monkey King. Otherwise not get close enough."

There was a long pause. I hadn't imagined it after all, even in my fevered situation. A shiver went down my innermost vertebrae.

Uncle Vesuvio looked at Granny. "Nobody can do a soul swap," he said uncertainly. "That's the last lost secret of Kenjo."

Granny Samurai clacked her teeth and grinned. "Not any more," she said.

One Last Thing to Do

Late Sunday afternoon I went back to the
zoo alone and found the porcupine's burrow.
I could hear Boris Hizzocks whimpering in
the darkness and I presented him with a list
of demands to which he must agree and then
I would help him get free from the quills and
we would never mention the incident again.

"Or else," I added, because now I firmly
had the upper hand and Boris
finally knew it. Stupid as he was,
he had seen enough to know I
was a true weirdo, and you don't
mess with
weirdos.

Here is a list of my top seven demands:

• No more insulting anyone in the class again.

• A recant of what happened in my garden so that I will no longer be wrongfully suspended and can be justly re-instated forthwith.

• A cessation of all torture, including Chinese burning and ear reddeners.

• No more biro puffs or spitting.

• No surprise visits to my house ever again.

• Removal to another seat so I can have a normal type of non-animal beside me in class.

• No speaking to me unless spoken to.

Sign here please: Date:
....

On Monday I went back to school and Uncle Vesuvio spoke stiffly to the headmaster, which he is excessively good at, and the headmaster made nice and I made some friends, which is also nice, and life continued.

I redistributed the stolen mobile phones and Boris never bullied anyone again.

Since then, because of my scribal abilities, Granny Samurai has engaged me to scribe a book for her, which she is calling THE LOST SECRET ART OF KENJO. You have been reading short extracts of it throughout this narrative, as advertising to whet your appetite for when it finally comes out.

"It will be a bestseller," predicts Granny Samurai, squishing the cold instant coffee between her teeth and ruminating on what she can and can't dictate to me. Some things are just too secret to write down. However, although six months have since gone by, there are no exact signs of it being finished yet. Nevertheless, we persevere.

"There are two types of author," wrote my Uncle Vesuvio recently, in a postcard from Kyrgyzstan, where he is on diplomacy once more. *"Those who start and those who finish. I am curious to see which one is Henrietta."*

"Blah blah blah yawn boring snoring," snorted Granny when I imparted his considered opinion to her. *"Vesuvio pluvio,"* she added, which is an ancient Latin insult and quite rude.

Why Did I Scribe This Story?

The story is nearly over. The careful reader will recall that at the beginning I said I would later on explain why I had started scribing it in the first place. Well here is why. I am a fanatic reader of books. Without books, there can be no readers. And without scribers, there can be no books. Also I am a great believer in doing everything once.

Granny Samurai, on the other hand, is dictating her book to make money. Good luck with that! Making books is nice, but I have read that there is hardly any money in it. In any case, I plan on being a scientist later on, or a Victorian. Victorians were victorious and wore hats. I like hats. They also liked uplifting stories with morals at the end. This is an uplifting story and you can find the moral on the next page. As well as being excessively moralistic, the Victorians were also pleased when people learnt things. Underneath the moral is a box where you can write what you have learnt. Goodbye.

Samuel Johnson
5 Summerhill Road
3 January 2013

The moral of the story is...

Be nice to grannies. Or else.

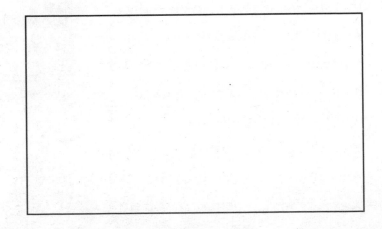

John Chambers was born and raised in Ireland. He has lived most of his life in big cities. He writes and draws for a living, working in a big, messy room watched by the mice and spiders. One day he would like to move to the country with his partner and their three children. The mice and the spiders may go with them. That's OK.

Samuel Johnson lives and scribes in the UK. You can find more of his scribal activities at: www.grannysamurai.com